# *Reagan's Reward*

Thousand Islands Brides
Book 3

By

# Susan G Mathis

smWordWorks
Fiction

Reagan's Reward by Susan G Mathis
Published by smWordWorks

ISBN: **978-0692686645**
Copyright © 2020 by Susan G Mathis
Cover design: Julia Evans
Editor: Denise Weimer

Available in print and e-book. For more information visit:
www.SusanGMathis.com

Visit her at www.SusanGMathis.com
sign up for her newsletter
and please
consider writing an Amazon review.
Thanks!

# PRAISE FOR REAGAN'S REWARD

As the third book of the Thousand Islands Brides series, I again found myself navigating the St. Lawrence River alongside an intriguing protagonist in her journey of love and self-discovery. There's something quite memorable and moving when experiencing history through story. Once again, Susan Mathis takes us back to the Gilded Age through a sensory tour of the breathtaking Thousand Islands straddling the US and Canadian border. Let's only hope Mathis continues to add more gems to this book series!—Jayme H. Mansfield - Award-winning author of *Chasing the Butterfly, RUSH,* and *Seasoned*

*Reagan's Reward,* set in 1912, is the third novella in Susan Mathis's series of the Thousand Islands Brides. This sweet love story sensitively addresses the attitudes and relationships between people of different faith backgrounds. The history and setting of the Thousand Islands, between the border of the U.S. and Canada, made me want to learn more about this fascinating area.—Janet Grunst, author of *A Heart Set Free, A Heart For Freedom, Setting Two Hearts Free*

Susan G Mathis has done it again with another touching story set in the Thousand Lakes region. With impeccable historical research, a setting she obviously knows well, and characters to cheer for, *Reagan's Reward* is a story I couldn't put down.— Donna Schlachter, author of historical mysteries including *Double Jeopardy* and *Kate*

Lovers of romance in historical settings will be delighted by the tender romance between Reagan and Daniel at Casa Blanca, an elaborate summer mansion in the famous Thousand Islands. Mathis has a gift for transporting the reader back in history to witness the lives of the very wealthy and their servants during the early twentieth century. As with all of Mathis' books, I've enjoyed learning about the real people and places that shaped our history during an era of opulence in the United States.—Marilyn Turk, award-winning author of *Abigail's Secret*

Susan Mathis paints such vivid settings. She pulled me into the early twentieth century on the St. Lawrence River and took my hand as we walked about Cherry Island with Reagan and Daniel. A sweet romance with a strong inspirational thread. This is a wonderful, curl up on the couch with hot chocolate kind of read.—Cindy Ervin Huff, 2019 Selah Finalist, author, and blogger

In *Reagan's Reward,* Susan Mathis skillfully crafted the story of Reagan Kennedy, a character introduced in *Devyn's Dilemma* (released April 2020). Once again, Mathis created historical fiction that blesses readers with her characterizations, storyline, and inspirational insights. Careful research and accurate details transport the reader back in time to a believable fictionalization of life at Casa Blanca, on Cherry Island, in the St. Lawrence River in 1912. *Reagan's Reward* is a delightful read and a welcome extension of the characters and story of *Devyn's Dilemma.*—Judy Keeler, co-author of *Meandering Among the Thousand Islands*

From the first sentence of *Reagan's Reward*, I was eager to learn what would happen to the young governess on her way to Cherry Island. Reagan Kennedy little suspects the daunting task that awaits her or the transformational power of faith and love. This Christmas novella opens the door to magnificent detail of America's Gilded Age in the Thousand Islands of 1912, giving readers access to the lives of the wealthy who vacationed there and the servants who worked to smooth the way.—Davalynn Spencer, award-winning author of *An Improper Proposal*

*Reagan's Reward* is a charming story set in an enchanting location. The hero and heroine are both characters to admire, and the rascally twins added plenty of excitement. This story was a delight to read.—Vickie McDonough, best-selling author of 50 books and novellas, including the *Texas Boardinghouse Brides* series.

Hold onto your fedora or bonnet for the journey will take us through rough waters beset by past abuses, waffling faith, and deceit, plus the antics of young twin boys. When the characters begin to face their challenges, they open their hearts, but we will have long since welcomed them into ours.—Carol Heilman, author of *Agnes Hopper Shakes Up Sweetbriar*

# **DEDICATION**

To my wonderful daughter, Janelle, who inspires me
with her zest for life and has blessed me with four
precious granddaughters, Reagan, Madison, Devyn, and
Peyton. Each one of you is a gift from heaven.

And especially to Reagan whose creative, adventurous,
lovable personality inspired the character of the same
name.

# ACKNOWLEDGMENTS

I hope you enjoy *Reagan's Reward.* If you've read any of my other books, you know that I love introducing history to my readers through fictional stories. I hope this story sparks interest in our
amazing past, especially the fascinating past of the marvelous Thousand Islands.

Thanks to Nancy and Phil for your warm hospitality and the mounds of information that I used to make this story so interesting. In researching Casa Blanca, I got to spend several days on Cherry Island, writing in the very spot where the story takes place and imagining my characters interacting there.

Thanks to you, my readers, for your faithful support and for staying connected.

Thanks to Judy Keeler, my wonderful historical editor who combs through my manuscripts for
accuracy. Because of her, you can trust that my stories are historically correct.

Thanks to my fabulous editor, Denise Weimer, for being the mentor I've always dreamed of and for sharing your talents with me.

To my amazing beta readers Laurie and Barb, for all your hard work and wise input, thank you.

To my husband, Dale, who even while in heaven, inspires my heroes because you will always be my hero.

To my many writer friends who so willingly write endorsements and reviews, encourage me in my writing, and pray for me. There are too many to name here, but you know who you are. Thank you.

And to all my dear friends who have journeyed with me in my writing. Thanks for your emails, social media posts, and especially for your reviews. Most of all, thanks for your friendship.

And to God, from whom all good gifts come. Without You, there would never be a dream or the ability to fulfill that dream. Thank you!

Please stay in touch at susan@susangmathis.com.

# Chapter 1

**June, 1912**

Reagan Kennedy scanned the dock for the boat that
would take her to Cherry Island and her new position as
governess at the Bernheim family's summer estate, Casa
Blanca. She was ready for this new adventure, anxious
even. Several vessels came into the Alexandria Bay harbor
and docked, but none for her. "Where is he?"

"Who, miss?" A woman twice her size stopped as
she passed by the bench where Reagan sat. She held a
parasol aloft and wore a hat with a beautiful peacock

feather so large that it kept bumping up against the parasol.

"Pardon. I didn't mean to speak aloud." Reagan blinked, noticing she'd been clutching the handles of her carpetbag a little too tightly. She willed her hands to relax. "The boatman from Casa Blanca should have been here hours ago. I fear he might've forgotten or I might have mixed up the meeting time."

"Not to worry. We Alexandria Bay residents are a neighborly lot, so someone will take you there if he doesn't show." The woman patted Reagan's shoulder gently with a lacey, gloved hand.

"Thank you for your concern. Patience ceases to be a virtue in my life all too often these days." Reagan sighed at her confession.

After leaving the Bournes' employ on Dark Island to care for her injured father, mother, and youngest sister last summer, Reagan had found serving them more burdensome than she could ever have imagined. Mother had fallen into a deep depression, and Father wasn't right in the head—speaking nonsense, scolding, belittling more often than not. And her three sisters were unwilling pupils even though her father demanded she teach and they learn. Yes, her patience had been tried over and over until the invitation to serve as governess became her ticket out. The question was, could she be patient with little boys?

"Then I shall pray you learn it well this summer, miss. Good day to you." The woman inclined her head as she turned toward town.

"And to you, ma'am. Much obliged." Reagan relaxed under the kindness of the lady's words and determined to sit and wait until nightfall if she had to.

From behind a large sailing ship, a small skiff came into view. A handsome boatman called out to her. "Miss Reagan Kennedy? Is that you?"

She acknowledged him with a nod, so he smiled as he pulled the skiff up to the dock, mooring it securely as she hopped up and hurried to him. His curly, ebony hair glistened in the sun like her mother's patent-leather shoes. His thick eyebrows and long, narrow sideburns matched his hair perfectly. His eyes did, too, as if they've been dyed that color.

When he straightened, he reached for her carpetbag and plopped it in the vessel. Then he held out his large hand to help her. She took it, a mixture of strength and warmth flowing through it as she stepped into the boat. Then she realized he was more than a full head taller than her. His broad shoulders and solid frame dwarfed her.

"Thank you. I've been waiting the entire afternoon." *Oops! That didn't sound very nice.*

The man glanced at her. "Aye. Pleased to meet you, lass. I'm Daniel Lovitz, Casa Blanca's boatman and all-around handyman." He barely gave her a glance. Instead, a muscle in his jaw twitched.

*Goodness! Better to make a friend than a foe.* "Thank you, sir, for fetching me, Mr. Lovitz. I didn't mean to offend. Merely to explain my nervousness. I feared I might be there all night."

"Ach. No offense taken, and please, call me Daniel. We'll be working together on a wee bit of an island and needn't worry about such formalities. And do forgive the wait. I had a rotten bit of luck and was unavoidably delayed." He untied the boat as he gave her a sideways glance. "Two mischievous boys await your care, and one

15

frustrated, sickly missus will be keen to see you." Finally, he gave her a wide-toothed grin that lit up his entire face.

"And you may call me Reagan." She settled into the skiff as Daniel eased out into the bay. "The missus is sick? Dear me. Whatever is the matter?"

Daniel rowed toward the main shipping channel of the St. Lawrence River. "Headaches besiege her. When they do, a dark room, quiet, and a cold cloth are all that help. Poor woman." His concern furrowed his brow.

"And the twins whom I am to care for? What about them?" Maybe she could squeeze some more information from Daniel before meeting the boys.

"Jacob and Joseph are the nephews of Mr. Bernheim, children of his sister. They are visiting for the summer."

"You mentioned they were mischievous?"

16

"They are boys. I expect that since they spend most of their time in a strict Jewish school in New York City, they want to sow a few wild oats while on the island. Be forewarned, they can get into trouble in two shakes of a lamb's tail." Daniel chuckled and continued to row.

Reagan shook off his caution. How bad could two little boys be? Then she pointed to the engine on the stern. "Might I ask why you aren't using the motor?"

Daniel glanced toward the back of the boat. "I deem the outboard motor to be for emergencies only. I like to row. It keeps me fit, but this Evinrude can get us out of any bind quickly if need be."

Neither spoke for several minutes until they were in the main shipping channel of the mighty St. Lawrence and parallel to a huge cargo ship that overwhelmed Reagan with its size. Daniel appeared unfazed by the massive freighter. Once the ship passed, she relaxed and fell to musing.

What would this summer hold for her? Miss Marjorie Bourne's telegram only said that the Bernheim family needed a governess to care for eight-year-old twin boys for the summer on one of the Thousand Islands. She'd jumped at the chance since she always wanted to be a teacher and loved passing on knowledge even more than she had enjoyed her previous work as a lady's maid to Miss Marjorie at The Towers castle on Dark Island.

What would this new family, this new position be like?

"Have you worked on the island long?" Reagan scanned the dozens of islands just a few hundred yards on either side of them.

Daniel's deep baritone voice held a tint of sadness. "I took over the caretaker position two summers ago after my father passed."

Reagan frowned. "I'm sorry for your loss. Is Cherry Island a fair distance from here?"

Daniel nodded. "Thank you. The island's not far from the bay. In fact, it's just around the bend."

Reagan itched to ask about so much more than she was likely to get from this man. His demeanor seemed more like a solicitor's rather than what she might have expected from an easygoing boatman's. He was clean-shaven and impeccably dressed in his dark trousers and vest and starched white shirt. Besides, he had the straightest, most aristocratic nose she'd ever seen. Yet solicitors usually didn't have bulging muscles as he did. Her cheeks grew warm until she put her hands on her face to cool them.

"Aye, over yonder is Cherry Island." With a dip of his chiseled chin, he pointed her toward a gleaming, white mansion sitting on the tip of the island. "That is Casa Blanca, home to Mr. and Mrs. Henry Bernheim, and the missus's father, Mr. Luis Marx, who is now in Cuba on business. Mrs. Mary Marx Bernheim, daughter of the famous Luis Marx, is the mistress of this grand retreat. The Pullmans built the original part of the house before the Marx family bought and expanded it."

More silence before Daniel pointed in the opposite direction, across the channel, where another huge cargo ship passed by. "Our neighbors are Florence Pullman and her husband, Frank Lowden. It was there on Pullman Island that President Ulysses S. Grant came to visit back in 1872. Thanks to that grand event, we Thousand Islanders have lots of neighbors now."

Maybe he wasn't as tightlipped as she had thought. He continued to pull at the oars until he brought the skiff all the way around the island to a large, two-story, wood-framed boathouse. A small balcony that appeared to be part of a residence jutted out over the lower level, which held several boats.

Daniel pointed to the upper portion as he pulled up to the long wooden dock. "I live up there." He paused as he moored the skiff. "Welcome to Cherry Island. I hope you will enjoy your stay here."

Once he secured the boat, he reached out to help her out of the boat. To her surprise, his touch was tender. Gentle.

"Thank you, sir." Reagan curtsied and gifted him with a wide smile.

From the dock, she could see nothing but a hilly island with lots of foliage. "But where am I to go now?"

Daniel chuckled a rumbling, deep sound that sounded like an ocean wave. "Ach. Forgive me. I will lead you up to the main house. It's this way."

The giant of a man took her carpetbag, and they followed the path through the center of the island. Beautiful, blossoming hydrangea and snowball viburnum bushes hedged the way, with a variety of flowering plants here and there. The fragrance filled her senses with delight.

Reagan's heart sped up with every step, and the lack of information nearly overwhelmed her. "Who am I to report to?"

"Mrs. Rosenstein is the head housekeeper. I'm not sure who your direct supervisor will be in such a circumstance as being governess to nephews." At that moment, he grinned and shrugged, looking like a little boy.

"No matter. It will all be sorted out presently." She sucked in a deep breath as they ascended the stairs to the screened door of a back porch. Daniel gave three quick taps on the wooden frame and stepped back. After what seemed like an eternity, a plump, matronly woman with black hair pulled into a tight bun answered.

"Mrs. Rosenstein, this is Miss Reagan Kennedy, the boys' governess." Daniel handed Reagan her bag and gave a quick, stiff bow. "I'll leave you two ladies to get acquainted." He gave Reagan a lopsided grin. "Keen to meet you, miss."

The housekeeper opened the door wider and stepped aside. "Welcome to Casa Blanca. The family is having an early supper, so I will take you to meet them. Follow me."

Reagan left her bag by the back door and followed her through the long, narrow kitchen, down a seemingly endless hallway, and into a roomy space. The elegant dining room, with its dark, wood trim and intricate, pressed-tin ceiling and walls, held a beautiful table, sideboard, and lots of silver and crystal. Though there were enough wicker-backed chairs to seat a dozen, only two were currently occupied.

Mrs. Rosenstein curtsied and Reagan followed her lead. "Good afternoon, Mr. and Mrs. Bernheim. This is Miss Kennedy, your new governess." With that, the housekeeper left Reagan standing alone, quivering in her boots.

Mr. Bernheim cast a wary gaze on her that caused her heart to thump even faster. He had perfectly combed, ink-black hair and a tidy mustache. His finely molded features included gray eyes that seemed to assess everything and thin lips that remained pressed together. He slipped off his spectacles. "Welcome. Sit, please." He motioned to her to take a chair across from them, between two empty chairs. "You will take meals with us, sitting between the twins and helping them as needed."

Reagan dipped her head as she took her seat, and the missus smiled kindly. Mrs. Bernheim appeared to be not much older than Reagan. She was small, beautiful. Glamorous, even. Her dark, curly hair was cut fashionably short, and she dressed in the latest style even for an early family dinner. "I'm glad you're here. I've been so anxious to employ help with the boys." Then she scanned the stairs, a spark of alarm lighting her dark-brown eyes. "Where are the boys? The maid should have brought them down by now."

Her husband answered, a hint of anger tainting his words. "I haven't seen them since breakfast. That maid better be seeing to them and those rascals had better not be causing trouble, or they will answer to me."

25

With a huff, he rang a bell to summon one of the kitchen maids to fetch the boys from upstairs. Within moments, the girl came down the front stairs just off the dining room and tiptoed toward the grand table, clasping her hands before her. "Pardon, but neither boy is upstairs anywhere. Shall I look outside?"

Mr. Bernheim shook his head and cast his eyes on Reagan. "Their governess can find them. You are dismissed."

The kitchen maid gave a quick curtsy and fled the room.

Mr. Bernheim clicked his tongue. "There's no time like the present to meet the boys. Go and find them, and bring them back as quickly as you can."

Reagan stood, nodded, and curtsied. "Yes, sir." She left by way of the kitchen and asked Mrs. Rosenstein,

"Where shall I find the boys, ma'am? I am tasked to do so but don't know the island."

The housekeeper rolled her eyes. "They could be anywhere, knowing them. Look to the trees, the rocks, wherever young boys might make sport or hide themselves."

Very helpful. Suppressing her frustration, Reagan exited onto the porch. She quickly scanned the small island, assessing two small wooden buildings to her left, one labeled *Ice House* and the other *Laundry House*. She checked both to no avail, but as she turned toward the pathway leading back to the boathouse, she spotted Daniel lurking behind a large bush.

She rushed to his side. "Daniel? Have you seen the boys?"

He put his finger to his lips and pointed toward a big tree about ten feet away and too near the shore.

27

Laughter drifted from a branch that hung over the river—where two boys sat, swinging their legs!

Reagan clasped her hands to her chest. "Oh, my gracious!" Her heart raced, and nervous perspiration wet her brow.

Daniel whispered to her, "I'll lay odds this is Jacob's doing. Joseph merely follows his lead." Frowning, he stepped out from behind the bush and approached the tree, calling out in a firm tone. "What are you two scrappy leprechauns doing? Get down here at once! You could fall to your deaths!"

Reagan followed him, pasting on her sternest face as she stared up at the twins.

The bigger of the two shrugged. "We climb trees all the time in the city. Papa lets us and mama has no say. Besides, you're not our boss."

Daniel stepped closer, his face red and his voice taut with anger. "But I am your elder. Your governess is here, and your uncle asks you to come at once. They will reckon with you."

The smaller boy bit his lip a moment, then spoke. "Come, Jacob. Master Daniel is right." He started to shimmy across the branch, but Jacob grabbed his arm. Joseph shook off his brother's grasp and scooted to the safety of the trunk.

Jacob wrinkled his freckled nose at them and turned to his brother. "We don't have to obey him—or her. He's just a boatman, and she's a *girl*. Besides, *we* are Bernheims, you 'fraidy-cat!!"

Daniel hurried over to the branch where Joseph sat. "Jump, Joseph. I'll catch you."

Joseph snapped a look toward his brother, but before Jacob could respond, Joseph jumped into Daniel's arms. He set him on the ground and turned to Jacob.

Reagan sighed. One down. One to go.

Jacob held tight to the tree. "You baby! You scaredy-cat! You'll never be the man I am!" With that, he turned his back on them and sat like a panther on his perch. If he had a tail, it would be swishing.

His eyes wide with fear, Joseph whined. "Please, Jacob. You know how Uncle is, and you might get hurt."

"Leave me be. I'll be down when I'm good and ready." Jacob didn't look at them as he spoke. His shoulders sagged as he stubbornly folded his arms in front of him. How he balanced on that branch was a mystery to Reagan.

Daniel bent down and whispered to Joseph. "You go ahead up to the house and don't worry about your brother, laddie. I'll make sure he's safe. He'll be there soon."

Joseph thanked Daniel before hurrying up to Casa Blanca. Should she accompany Joseph or wait with Daniel? She decided on the latter.

She and Daniel pretended to stroll to the boathouse but instead hid behind a large lilac bush and watched Jacob carefully, ready to run to his aid if he needed it. But apparently, he didn't, for in only minutes, he scrambled down the tree and hurried back to the house as if he hadn't a care in the world.

"That's one way to meet the boys." Reagan rolled her eyes, then brushed off her skirt. "I thank you for your help, for fetching me from the bay, and for being my first Cherry Island friend."

Daniel grinned. "'Tis no problem, lass."

She propped a hand on her hip. "Good, because something tells me I might need a little help now and then."

## Chapter 2

A friend? But they were barely acquainted. The possibility of allowing Reagan a spot in his life made Daniel draw up short, rubbing his chin as he watched her hurry back into the house.

Who was this wee bit of a thing who came to do battle with imps such as Jacob and Joseph? He shuddered at the anger he'd felt toward Jacob just then. Indeed, he could have slapped the boy! Aye, the lovely lass might be in for a rude awakening when she took charge of those two.

And yet ... those silvery-blue eyes might very possibly drill a hole into them. They had nearly melted him as he rowed the skiff and again distracted him as he tried to deal with the twins. Thankfully, her fine, feminine features softened the blow of her piercing gaze. And then there were her pale-pink lips. Never before had his heart danced a jig as it had during those moments with her in the skiff.

Indeed, she was a rare beauty, yet so tiny that he was certain he could pick her up with one arm. Could she be a match for the twins? He wasn't so sure.

Daniel headed to the icehouse, his original destination before the boys had diverted him. Opening the heavy door, he sucked in the refreshing coolness. He nearly closed it but left the door ajar to let in just enough light to see what he needed to do. Once his eyes adjusted to the dark inside, he grabbed the pick and began chopping a block of ice small enough to fit in his boathouse icebox.

Suddenly, the door swung wide, and light flooded the icehouse. "There you are, darling!"

Etta. Why wouldn't she leave him be?

Daniel pasted on an insincere smile. "Good afternoon, Etta. May I help you?"

She closed the door within an inch or two, and darkness again shadowed the room. "Oh, I just wanted a chunk of ice to quench my thirst. My, but it's cold in here." She came toward him and wrapped her arms around him. "Keep me warm. Please?"

Was the woman crackers? Daniel wrenched away from her and stepped back, bumping his shin against a sharp edge of ice. Ignoring the pain, he reached for the door and opened it wide. "Ach. This is inappropriate, miss. We shouldn't be in here alone. Nor should we embrace so. Nor should you call me 'darling.'"

Etta gave him a tantalizing gaze as she smoothed her bodice. "But we are friends, are we not? What's wrong with that?"

He'd get his ice later. "I must go. Good day." As fast as his feet could take him, Daniel rushed back to the boathouse, heart racing, but not with pleasure as it had with Reagan. With disgust. How could a fine Jewish lady's maid act so brazenly? And how could Mrs. Bernheim have chosen such a woman to serve her?

The story of Delilah entered his mind, and he reached up and ran his hand through his hair. Surely, Etta wasn't the vixen Delilah was. But her actions spoke volumes. She'd pursued him relentlessly these past few weeks, ever since she arrived on the island with the

Bernheims. Oh, at first it was friendly chit-chat. But a touch here, a flirtation there, and each day brought more and more uncomfortable, inappropriate contact with her. He'd begun avoiding her, taking a different path whenever he spied her afar off not frequenting the places she seemed to prefer.

Upon entering his apartment, Daniel consulted the clock on the mantel. He'd promised to help the twins fish that evening, and they'd be there in less than an hour. Would the lovely Reagan accompany them? The notion made his stomach flip, but he needed to eat, and quickly. He ate the leftovers from last night and chugged a large glass of lukewarm water. If only he had the ice he'd gone for.

After running water to soak the dishes in the sink, Daniel hurried downstairs to load the poles and prepare the skiff for their outing.

Before long, Joseph's soft voice beckoned him from around the corner. "Mr. Daniel? Are you there?"

"I'm coming." He rounded the corner of the boathouse, and his heart leapt, for Reagan indeed trailed behind the twins.

"Boys. Miss Kennedy. What a pleasure to have the three of you join me on our fishing adventure. I hope our time will agree with you, miss."

Reagan's eyes widened. "Oh, I love to fish! Miss Marjorie Bourne, my former mistress from Dark Island, upriver, took me fishing many times while in her employ."

Daniel took a step back. "Well, now, that is a surprise. Most women find it undesirable."

Reagan shook her head. "Not I. How about you, boys? Do you like to fish?" Her tone enthusiastic, she put a hand on her hip and leaned down toward them.

Joseph shrugged. "I like to ride in the boat and see the ships more."

Jacob rolled back on his boot heels, snapping his suspenders. "I love fishing. It's manly."

Reagan's tinkling-bell giggle reminded Daniel of his mother's laugh. He missed that sound. He missed *her*.

"Well, the skiff is ready. The poles are loaded, so let's go." Daniel helped the boys into the boat and secured them with life vests.

Jacob pulled at the bulky contraption. "I hate this thing. I can swim." He tried to pull it off, but Daniel stopped him.

"You must leave it on. Uncle's orders."

Jacob squirmed away, slanting Daniel a narrow-eyed glare. He plunked down on Joseph's bench and gave him a shove. "Move over."

"Ouch! Your elbows are sharp." Joseph scooted away from his brother.

Reagan shook her finger at them. "Now, boys. Let's be gentlemen. Get along, or we mightn't have another outing like this in the near future."

Jacob wrinkled his nose, lodging his objection. But he didn't voice it.

After shoving off from the dock, instead of heading toward the shipping channel, Daniel turned the boat toward the American mainland. "This time of the evening, fish tend to feast closer to shore. Let's see what we can find there."

Reagan pointed to a tiny island just off the dock— barely larger than Casa Blanca's living room. "Does that belong to the Bernheims?"

Daniel snapped his chin toward it. "It does. It's called Little Angel Isle, but it's seldom used. There are lots of tree roots under that water, so it's rather dangerous. You laddies take care and don't go over there, aye?"

Joseph nodded, but Jacob just stared at him. What was the imp thinking? He'd have to watch that one!

Reagan was studying the rest of Cherry Island, her face angelic.

"Do you know of the famous Abraham & Strauss and Macy's Department Store in New York City?"

Reagan blinked, her brows furrowed.

He tilted his head toward shore. "These are the Strauss and the Abrahams summer cottages. People call them the Twin Cottages, though they aren't identical. Mrs. Bernheim's aunt and uncle are Mr. and Mrs. Nathan Strauss, and his business partner is Mr. Abraham. They built their cottages back in 1899."

Reagan lifted her hand to her chest, her face paling, even in the evening sunshine. "I do! Such famous people. I think the Bournes may have hosted them at a party once on Long Island."

"Yes, well, many of the wealthy New York City lot have built summer homes here in the past few decades. Some hail from Rochester and other cities too. This seems the place to be these days to get away from the heat of the city."

"When are we going to fish? The sun will set before you two stop talking." Jacob folded his arm in front of his chest and pursed his lips.

"In a moment, laddie." He tossed him a warning scowl before motioning to a nearby cove. "I believe some perch and bass might be looking for a meal over yonder."

Soon, Daniel dropped anchor, pinned a worm on each of the boys' hooks, and handed their poles to them. "Next time, you'll need to bait your own hooks. Now be patient and quiet."

Reagan sat forward as though she was waiting for something.

"Would you like to try using my pole, miss?" Surely, she'd watch, not fish, but Daniel had to offer out of politeness.

"Please. And I can bait my own hook." Reagan giggled again. His mother's giggle. Despite his consternation at her theft of his fishing opportunity, his heart warmed.

Daniel handed her the pole and the jar of worms and watched her fearlessly bait her hook, biting the tip of her tongue and scrunching up her nose in concentration. Adorable. When she finished, a glimmer of accomplishment twinkled in her eyes.

"Well done, lass!" Daniel beamed, rewarding her with a slight bow. He almost winked but held it back with much restraint. No need to scare her off as surely as Etta did him.

"Why, thank you." Her lips pressed into a smirk, Reagan swiveled on the bench and dropped her line into the deep water.

"I got one! I got one!" Joseph squealed and yanked on his line with all his strength, nearly tipping the skiff.

"Sit still or you'll turn us over! Slow and steady. Reel it in slowly." Daniel slid next to Joseph and helped him bring in a fair-sized sunfish. The little boy's excitement filled the atmosphere, his grin wide and pleased.

Reagan winked at the child. "You got the first fish of the day, Joseph. Congratulations!"

"Thank you, ma'am."

"It was beginner's luck, that's all." Jacob's jealousy oozed from his words. "I'll get a bigger one. Watch me. That's just a little nothing fish."

Should Daniel scold him or let his governess correct him?

~ ~ ~

Before Reagan could address Jacob's unkind words, a strong tug came on her line. "Oh my! I think I've got something." She gave it a quick yank to set the hook and began reeling it in, her pole straining under the weight.

Daniel straightened. "Might be a bass or even a pike. Hold steady, miss. Need help?"

She shook her head, bit her lip, and reeled, pulling with all her might. "I can do it, I think."

"A girl. A girl fishing?" Jacob grumbled as he batted his pole in the water, splashing his brother and her.

"Sit still, Jacob." Daniel placed a hand on the boy's knee, and his steady gaze made her more and more nervous. Finally, she pulled a large northern pike up to the surface, and Daniel scooped it into a net.

"Haven't seen one this big yet this year. Well done, miss! Cook will be more than pleased. The Bernheims love fresh pike." Daniel grinned, and Reagan warmed under his compliment.

"I'm next, and I'll get one even bigger. You'll see." Jacob slapped the water with his pole again, harder this time. "Come on, fish. Where are you?"

"You'll not catch a fish like that. You mustn't not disturb the water, or you'll scare them away. Have patience, lad." Daniel stroked Jacob's back, but the child squirmed away from his touch.

Jacob narrowed his eyes, his foot beating out an impatient rhythm.

"If you tap the skiff like that, the fish will scatter. Settle down, child, and I'll help."

"I don't need your help!" Jacob cast both Daniel and Reagan a glare.

"I got another!" Joseph pulled in a small yellow perch this time. "He's just a baby. Should he go back to his mama?"

"Yes, Joseph. That'd be the right thing to do." Reagan breathed a sigh at the boy's kind heart.

"Stupid fish. Where are you?" Jacob nearly howled as he whirled around. "This isn't fun. Let's go home." He threw his pole into the skiff and pouted, arms tightly wrapped around his middle.

"It's all right, Jacob. You'll get a whopper next time. I just know you will." Reagan tried to console the boy, clapping his shoulder. But he pushed her away.

"Don't touch me. You're just a girl." He gave her a look that would melt a statue, but Daniel grabbed hold of his arm.

"You may not talk that way to your governess. Or any lady. That is not how a gentleman speaks to a woman."

"My father does, so I can too." Jacob turned his back to them, stiff and proud.

Regret twisted Reagan's heart . . . and something else. Dread? What unhealthy relationships would she face at Casa Blanca, and could she, a mere servant, stand up to them? She had to try. "Mr. Daniel is correct. No gentleman should demean a lady with his words." Noticing a spark of anger remained in Daniel's eyes, Reagan cautioned the man in a whisper. "Give him time. I'll work with him. He'll come around."

Once they returned to the dock, a woman with dark, striking features and a curvy figure stood there waiting for them. She glared at Reagan. "Where have you been? The missus wanted the boys in bed by now. She'll be mighty vexed."

Reagan defended herself, even before knowing who the woman was. "It's not yet eight o'clock. I thought their bedtime was at nine."

The woman tossed her a scowl before rolling her eyes. "Little you know." She faced Daniel. "Are you leading *her* astray?"

Daniel held a hand up to stop the banter. He helped the three of them out of the skiff and tugged the boys out of their vests. Without a *thank you*, Jacob took off running toward the house.

"Miss Reagan Kennedy, this is Miss Etta Damsky, Mrs. Bernheim's maid. You'd better skedaddle. I'll take care of the skiff and the fish. Good evening to you."

Reagan curtsied. "Good evening, sir. And thank you for the fishing adventure."

Daniel acknowledged her then cast a wary eye toward Etta.

Etta picked up her skirts and turned, but not before batting her eyelashes in Daniel's direction. "Good night, Daniel."

Reagan took Joseph's hand and headed toward the house, following Etta as she clipped along the path. The child piped up. "I caught a fish, Miss Etta."

"Did you, now? I despise the sport. It's such a dirty, *man's* sport."

"Miss Reagan caught a big one. Mr. Daniel said it was the biggest he'd seen this year!"

50

Etta turned, and her eyes narrowed into tiny slits. Then she sniggered. "Such an unladylike thing to do. I've never …" She paused, and a mischievous grin crossed her pretty pink lips. "I've heard tales about you. I hope they aren't true."

"What tales?" Reagan couldn't believe the boldness of this woman. Who was she to challenge her, a stranger?

"Oh, just this and that. Well, ta-da. I must attend to my mistress, a task I much prefer to yours, trying to handle these wild boys." She wiggled her fingers, hurrying up the pathway without a backward glance.

Of all the nerve!

Reagan shook herself from her frustration and turned to Joseph. "I'm proud of you. That was quite a catch. Two in one day!"

Joseph squeezed her hand and looked up at her, smiling. "Thank you. I think I'm going to like you."

"Well, that's good, because I already like you—and your brother." Hopefully, she added that last bit without too much of a falter. And hopefully, it would be true soon. "I know we'll have a memorable summer together." And she prayed that would be true, for sure.

Joseph led her onto the veranda, through the door, and into the living room, heading straight to the intricately carved main staircase. As they climbed the stairs, Reagan looked for signs of Jacob. "Where do you think your brother is?"

Joseph shrugged. "Oh, he's probably on his bed, sulking. He does that a lot."

Reagan stifled a laugh. "He may act angry, but we can guess he's really disappointed at not catching a fish. We must be charitable, mustn't we?"

"Yes, but he's always sulking about something or other. Or he's being mean. Or sneaky. Or naughty. Depends on the day. Or hour." Joseph spoke not in judgment but as if it were a fact.

"Well, let's see if we can help him get past that, shall we?"

"It'd be easier for God to part the St. Lawrence than to make Jacob be nice." Again, no judgment darkened the little boy's tone.

Reagan stopped and bent down to Joseph's level. "God can do anything, including helping your brother."

Joseph nodded and turned the bedroom doorknob. Sure enough, Jacob lay face-down on the bed, wet, dirty clothes and all. Light-green walls made the room quite cheery. So did the twin beds bedecked with matching quilts. A mirrored dresser and sink completed the room.

"Let's get you boys ready for bed, shall we? Then, would you like a story or a prayer? What is your bedtime routine?"

"I don't need no girl to tuck me in. I'm no sissy." Jacob scrambled out of bed and put his hands on his hips. "But *he* is."

"Am not. You're a meanie." Joseph frowned as if wounded. He turned his back to his brother and addressed Reagan. "But I'd like a story. Mama always tells us a story before bed."

She stroked Joseph's shoulder. "Tell you what. You two wash your face and hands and put on your pajamas. Then I'll come back and tell you a whopper of a fish story."

Without waiting for Jacob to object, she slipped out the door and left them to their duties. She went to her room, just a few feet away, and assessed her surroundings.

Thank goodness, Mrs. Rosenstein had showed her the accommodations earlier that day, else she'd not know where to sleep!

The twin beds were shoved together into one huge bed, much larger than she'd ever need. She shook her head as she wondered how long it would take to make it each day. An adjoining bath at the far end of the pink room and visible from the doorway held a claw-foot shower. How curious! But the best part was the huge, picture widow that overlooked the main channel, where a ship passed by just then.

After about ten minutes, she returned to the boys' room, hoping they were in their beds. She knocked gently on the door and entered to find Joseph washed, clothed, and sitting in bed, hands folded, a welcoming smile on his face.

Jacob, however, still lay on his bed in his dirty clothes. Defiant.

"Do you need me to help you, Jacob? Can you not wash your own face and hands and dress yourself?" She took several steps toward him, and he hopped out of bed like a rabbit running from a fox.

"I'll do it myself." He splashed water on his face, barely touched his face with the towel, and scurried into his pajamas.

Oh well. That'd have to do for tonight.

"All right, then. Shall we hear about Jonah and his big fish?"

"Oh yes. We know that story." Joseph clapped with excitement. "But that fish was way bigger than mine. He was big enough to eat Jonah!"

"Not exactly eat him. But he swallowed him whole." Reagan tickled Joseph's tummy and turned to

Jacob in the bed next to him. "And you, my young man. Thank you for getting ready for bed so quickly." She ruffled his hair, and although Jacob motioned to sweep her hand away, he ducked his head to cover a twitch of a grin.

"So, boys, why did the whale swallow Jonah?"

Joseph answered as quick as a wink. "He was bad. He wouldn't obey Yahweh."

"Correct. Now I'll tell you the story from the beginning, and you can help along the way."

Once Reagan had finished the tale, she tucked both of the boys into bed and turned out the light. Returning to her room, she prayed. For the boys. For herself. And for the whales she might encounter this summer.

## Chapter 3

The next morning, Reagan followed two hungry boys to the breakfast table, attempting to keep them from hanging on the stairway railings or hopping the stairs two at a time. When they got to the bottom, Jacob jumped three stairs and landed with a loud *plunk*.

"Quiet, boys. Your aunt may not appreciate your racket." She patted their shoulders in a gentle warning.

Joseph gave her a scowl and a snort, surprising her. Had Jacob planted negative ideas about her?

Once seated at the dining room table with Mr. and Mrs. Bernheim, Reagan helped the twins set their napkins on their laps, and with a finger to her lips, gave them an affirming wink.

Without so much as a hello, Mr. Bernheim prayed, "Blessed are You, Lord our God, Ruler of the universe, who brings forth bread from the earth. Amen."

The rest of them echoed *amen*s and that was that. Mr. Bernheim took a sip of his coffee and studied each of the boys. Jacob's smirk told Reagan that his uncle didn't intimidate him in the least, while Joseph's beet-red ears revealed the opposite.

Finally, Mr. Bernheim took a bite of his fried potatoes and redirected his attention to Reagan. "Mrs. Bernheim tells me you were a lady's maid. Why on earth would you become a governess?" Mr. Bernheim eyed her with disdain. Now it was Reagan's turn to squirm.

"I ... I found that teaching is rather satisfying. First with teaching my lady's maid successor and then my three sisters."

Mr. Bernheim continued. "It is a step down, if you ask me. Why did you not return to service with the Bournes?"

The interrogation was embarrassing, especially in front of the boys. "The Bournes are traveling to Europe for the summer, and my parents forbade me to cross the ocean. Besides, Miss Marjorie had already employed a lady's maid, so she suggested I try my hand at teaching."

Mr. Bernheim harrumphed. "I hope you will be up to the task. And there will be none of your Christian religion. Is that understood?" Leaning forward, he set down his fork, as if to challenge her.

"Of course, Mr. Bernheim." After learning she'd be working for a Jewish family, her father had sternly warned her about this. He'd said she'd be dismissed if she spoke of her faith, and that if she were dismissed, she'd not bother returning home. Reagan cleared her throat and gazed around the room. "You have a wonderful home here. Thank you for having me." She glanced at the missus, who finally responded by speaking up.

"My parents bought Melrose Lodge from Emily Pullman in 1897. They added onto it until we now have twenty-seven rooms on three stories." A ghost of a smile danced around Mrs. Bernheim's lips. "My father, Mr. Luis Marx, and Mama made it what it is today. But since Mama died in this very house almost ten years ago, Father rarely visits here anymore."

Reagan tilted her head. "I'm sorry for your loss, ma'am."

"That was before we were born, Aunt." Joseph dropped a piece of his fatback, so Reagan retrieved it from the floor, tucking it under her plate.

"You are correct, nephew." Mrs. Bernheim's flat tone and sad eyes betrayed her loss.

During an uncomfortable silence, Reagan surveyed her surroundings—to her right, an elegant sideboard held sparkling silver and crystal galore. To her left, stained-glass transoms, and through the entry, the living room, kitchen hallway, and butler's pantry. "Your home is splendid, to be sure."

Mr. Bernheim responded, turning to his wife. "Perhaps it would be wise for you to give her a tour of the house and instructions where the children may and may not go." He gave the boys a narrow-eyed warning.

Mrs. Bernheim finished her tea. "I shall be glad to show her around."

Her husband nodded, picking up his paper and opening it. "Very well, then. But remember, I shall be leaving after the noon hour to catch the two o'clock train."

Mrs. Bernheim patted her lips and laid her napkin on the table. "I remember, *mein liba*. And I shall miss you."

"What's *mein liba*?" Joseph asked.

"It means *my love*." Mrs. Bernheim's cheeks turned rosy.

Jacob snickered into his napkin. Once the boys had finished their porridge and milk, the missus rose. "Shall we see the house, miss?" Without waiting for Reagan's response, Mrs. Bernheim waved her hand at the twins. "Boys, you go outside and play for a bit. But, mind you, don't get into mischief."

Reagan held back a grin as they scurried out onto the wrap-around veranda. Their aunt knew them well, it seemed. But could Reagan trust them to run off and play on their own under her watch? She doubted it.

Mrs. Bernheim took her elbow as if they were friends. "Let's start here." She pointed down the long hallway that led to the kitchen. Though Reagan had traversed it, she hadn't stopped to explore.

"Here's the butler's pantry. This Meissen blue-and-white china and beautiful canister set must not be touched by little hands. Neither should the Fostoria and Heisey glass nor the Czechoslovakian china my mother so lovingly collected through the years." She tossed Reagan a warning glance before turning to the opposite wall. "And here is the butler's electric pull station, a call box installed by W.T. Bascom. It shows the name of the room ringing for service. Please keep the boys from pressing any of the buttons."

Reagan assented as she glanced at glass-enclosed switches.

To the left of the call box, Mrs. Bernheim touched a closed door. "This is the wine cellar. We keep the door closed at all times. The boys have been warned not to enter as we have some rather expensive bottles inside."

"Yes, ma'am." Reagan followed her to the end of the hallway.

Entering the kitchen without interrupting the work of Cook and her maids, the missus pointed to a door on the far, left end of the kitchen that was slightly ajar. "That is the back stairs leading to the servants' quarters as well as to the second floor. The boys may use them as long as they don't disturb the staff."

"Of course, ma'am. I'll keep a good eye on them." Reagan dipped her head, trying to assure her mistress she understood her role.

They returned the way they came and entered the largest adjoining room. "This is our living room and reception hall. The walls and ceilings are pressed tin because it is a fire retardant." She tilted her chin up toward the transom over the three screen doors that led out to the veranda. "Notice the stained-glass fleur-de-leis. Are they not lovely? That is one of the many reasons the children mustn't play in here. There are many valuable decorations and collectables that must be kept safe."

French doors led to another room. Reagan moved closer and peeked inside to see two player pianos and a pump organ, then pointed to the transoms around five doors leading to the veranda. "Is this the music room? These stained-glass lyres are so beautiful! And five doors?"

Mrs. Bernheim took in a deep breath, her gaze radiant. "My favorite room. I usually play the piano in the evenings. The screen doors offer lovely river cross-breezes."

Reagan smiled. "It's stunning, and I love music."

Mrs. Bernheim turned, opening a door under the intricately carved staircase that revealed a small marble lavatory. "This is for guests only. Please have the children only use their bathroom upstairs. We don't want undue messes about the house. I would also like them to avoid playing in the reception hall, the kitchen, and the butler's pantry. And they must never, ever go into Mr. Bernheim's office." She motioned to a small office-library off the living room. "He would be most displeased."

The missus faced Reagan, her face taut with caution. "Regarding my husband, he will be leaving for a few days on business, but when he is home, the twins need not be under foot. He is not used to children, and his rules must be followed impeccably. Is that understood?"

Reagan curtsied to punctuate her affirmation. "Yes, ma'am."

"Furthermore, I tend to have bouts of headaches now and then. When they plague me, quiet is of the utmost importance. I've told the boys this, but I fear they may forget."

"I'm sorry for your pain. I will do my best to ensure they follow your instructions, missus."

Mrs. Bernheim touched Reagan's forearm. "I know you will, but they are a handful, to be sure." She paused and looked toward the veranda. "I believe we should continue our tour later. Their silence makes me nervous."

Reagan giggled. "I quite agree. Thank you for showing me around and for your instructions. I appreciate your time."

"Of course. We will continue with the two upper floors another time."

After bobbing a curtsy, she hurried out onto the veranda where she hoped to find Jacob and Joseph playing quietly and nicely.

Not likely. Where could those rascals be?

~ ~ ~

Daniel shoveled dirt onto the pathway that ran along the shore, filling in the ruts and holes made by a recent downpour. When Reagan scurried toward him, scanning the area presumably for her charges, his heart sped up. Stopping to raise a hand of welcome, he sucked in a breath when she flashed a grin at him.

"Top of the morning to you, my fair lass. Might you be looking for two leprechauns who happen to look like boys?"

Reagan giggled. He'd have to find ways to hear that sound regularly.

"I am. The missus has been giving me a tour and instructions about the house. Have you seen them?" She assessed the area behind him, but he took a teasing step to obstruct her view.

Daniel grinned. "I have, but their silence means trouble. Whenever wee boys get too quiet, there's likely mischief afoot." He turned and pointed toward the water's edge. "They should be just beyond the gazebo. Let me escort you to them."

He leaned his shovel on a hearty clump of lilacs, sending their scent into the air.

"The smell of lilacs. Are they not intoxicating?" Reagan closed her eyes, looking more like an angel than a girl.

Daniel waved a hand. "Aye. This way, miss."

She opened her eyes and looked at him as if she'd just awakened from a dream. She smiled, her lips parting ever so gently. He stumbled on the rocky path, catching himself in an embarrassed moment.

"Clumsy me. You tend to distract me, lass." Daniel cleared his throat. "The boys were playing with a frog just a bit ago."

"I haven't had the opportunity to be around little boys very often. I only had sisters, and we only played with girls. Any pointers?" Reagan bit her bottom lip, her silvery eyes eager under delicate, furrowed brows.

Daniel chuckled. "Aye, well, you're in for a rude awakening, I'm afraid. Not only are boys very different, these boys in particular will test your mettle. Especially that one." He motioned to Jacob, who was busy tormenting the frog with a stick. A deep pool with rock walls confined the helpless creature, and Jacob poked at the poor frog's underbelly. Joseph stood there silent, white as a sheet, looking as though he might lose his breakfast at any moment.

When Reagan saw what Jacob was doing, her face turned red, and she thrust her hands on her hips and stomped up to him. "Jacob. Stop that at once!" She grabbed the stick out of his hand and glared at the boy.

But Jacob only grinned at her.

"That is one of God's creatures. How dare you torture it?" She grasped the stick in both hands, breaking it in two and throwing it into the bushes with a huff. "Sit down. Both of you."

Daniel's own anger ebbed at how quickly Reagan took control of the situation. Jacob and Joseph plunked down on the grass. Jacob folded his arms and stared at the pool still holding the frog. Joseph looked like he was about to cry. Maybe this little spit of a thing could handle them after all.

"Did God not make this creature?" Her voice quivered. Neither boy answered as she bent down and picked up the frog, stroking it gently, tenderly. She held it up to her face, looking straight into its eyes as she cooed lovingly. "Hello, little fellow. I'm sorry you've had a bad day on account of these two boys. May God forgive them." She snapped a glare at the twins, causing Joseph to burst into tears and Jacob to squirm. "I shall let you go back to the freedom you deserve and ask your forgiveness for the suffering you endured. But first ..." She turned to the boys. "Do you have something to say to this fellow?"

Joseph sucked in a breath and whimpered. "I'm sorry, froggy."

Jacob pursed his lips, but his eyes betrayed him.

Reagan went over to Jacob and sat next to him, still cradling the frog. She unfolded the boy's arms and pried his hands open, placing the frog in his palms and gently holding it there. "Would you want someone to poke you with a stick, Jacob?"

Jacob's lips started to quiver, and his eyes brimmed with tears. Reagan waited, staring at the boy with such compassion that Daniel's own eyes prickled.

"Sorry, frog." Jacob began whimpering as he dropped the frog and watched it hop off into the water. The child threw his hands to his face, covering his eyes as he wept in contrition.

Reagan let both boys cry for several moments, rubbing their backs and mouthing what Daniel could only guess was a prayer. What kind of woman sat before him? Someone tender, wise beyond her years.

After several tense minutes, Joseph laid his head on Reagan's lap, and Jacob scooted closer to her, placing his head on her shoulder. She stroked Joseph's hair and put her arm around Jacob, who actually leaned into her ever so slightly. What a wonderful mother she'd make one day!

~ ~ ~

Reagan wiped the gravy off Joseph's face, and supper was done. He smiled his appreciation but then turned to his aunt, imploring her to set them free. "Thank you for supper. May we be excused, please, Aunt Mary?"

Mrs. Bernheim motioned toward the staircase. "You may. Go to your room and spend some time reading."

Jacob groaned as he stood and pushed in his chair a little too hard.

"Gently, Jacob. Those are very expensive Thonet chairs. From Vienna."

Jacob barely murmured an apology and fled up the stairs with his brother.

Mrs. Bernheim chuckled as she lifted the teacup to her lips. "Those two. So cute, but such energy!" She turned to Reagan. "Tell me about your previous experience here in the islands."

Reagan let out a tiny sigh. "As Miss Marjorie's lady's maid, I loved my time with the Bournes, both at their home on Long Island and at The Towers on Dark Island. I enjoyed seeing the massive ships pass by, as I do here, and found the castle to be a magical part of the world."

Mrs. Bernheim nodded. "It was Marjorie Bourne who recommended you so highly. You taught an untrained girl to be a lady's maid?"

"Yes. Devyn McKenna was a quick learner. It was easy, really."

"Becoming proficient as a lady's maid is never easy. I've been through several who were slow to learn, even after they were schooled in the art. You said you instructed your three younger sisters?"

Reagan shrugged. "Yes, while my parents recovered from the carriage accident, I occupied my sisters with book learning. Reading. Writing. Mathematics. History. And the Bible." Catching herself, she sucked in a breath.

Mrs. Bernheim looked straight into her eyes and cleared her throat. "We call the first five books the Torah, but you are wise to teach children God's words."

Reagan blinked. Did Mrs. Bernheim not consider it an error to speak of the Christian Bible, despite what her husband had said earlier?

"But you must take care, miss, when you teach my nephews. They are Jewish boys of conservative parents, and Mr. Bernheim would be displeased if you attempt to pass on your differing beliefs. He was reticent to have a Gentile governess in our employ." The missus paused, letting several uncomfortable moments of silence pass between them, so Reagan took a sip of her now lukewarm tea. "You may teach from the Torah, the Old Testament, but not from the New Testament. We cannot abide it."

"Yes, ma'am. Certainly." Reagan bit her bottom lip. "Shall I teach them about God's great creation? There's so much scope for learning of nature and its wonders here in the islands."

"Of course. But they must not while away their summer without daily reading, writing, and mathematics. Is that understood?" Mrs. Bernheim took a bite of a biscuit and set it back on her saucer.

"Absolutely. And art and music? I love to sketch and would be delighted to show them a few things. Yet I know little of music." Reagan's brow furrowed.

Mrs. Bernheim waved off her concern. "I shall tend to their piano lessons at four o'clock sharp every day. That is, when I don't have my headaches."

Reagan grinned. "Thank you, missus."

"Now go and tend to your charges." Mrs. Bernheim smiled, gesturing toward the grand staircase.

Reagan stood and curtsied. "Thank you for your wise counsel and for entrusting me with your nephews."

But could she be trusted to respect such restrictions, or would she slip up and endanger her future? Reagan pondered her predicament as she climbed the stairs to tend to the twins.

# Chapter 4

Reagan surveyed her room. Mrs. Rosenstein had said she'd chosen it since it was far from Mr. and Mrs. Bernheim's room. And since there had never been any Bernheim children, no nursery or playroom existed. Besides, much of their learning would be done outside, anyway. Such a large bedroom would work just fine as a makeshift classroom. With much excitement and a bit of trepidation, she prepared for her first day of class.

The white, pressed-tin ceiling gave the room a bright, airy feel, and though the boys would likely not appreciate the pink walls, she liked them. Her large bed faced the large picture window. The deep alcove sported the window and held two desks for the twins as well as a small table and chair to serve as her teacher's desk. With the side windows open, the cross-breeze cooled the room well. On one wall hung a chalkboard with a near-empty bookshelf below it.

She set two precious *McGuffy Reader*s on each desk just as a huge cargo ship passed by the island, filling the picture window with an awe-inspiring sight—so close she would see men working on its deck. Perhaps she'd have to turn the desks away from the window, else she mightn't be able to keep the twins' attention.

She picked up a piece of chalk and wrote on the board, *Welcome to Casa Blanca Primary School. I trust we'll have a fine time of learning together. ~Miss Reagan.* She sneezed. Chalk always made her sneeze. She wiped the dust from her hands, remembering how much she disliked the feel of it.

A knock on the door beckoned her to start school. Her first day as a paid teacher. Ready or not, here they come! "Come in, boys."

Joseph entered first, a huge grin and twinkling eyes revealing his excitement. Jacob shuffled in, shoulders sagging, with a grumpy frown, mumbling to his brother. "Why do we have to do school? And with a girl? Girls are dumb. Girls shouldn't be teachers."

Best to pick her battles carefully, so she chose to ignore the comment. "Welcome, Jacob and Joseph. Please have a seat at your desks. It's a lovely day, is it not?"

Joseph snapped her an affirming glance as he slipped into a desk, but Jacob grabbed his brother's desk and shook it. "That's my desk, sissy. I want to sit nearest the window."

"I sat here first. It's mine." Joseph stood his ground, albeit not too confidently.

Jacob rattled Joseph's desk violently.

"That's enough. Joseph will sit there today, and tomorrow you can use that desk. Then we'll switch every other day. How does that sound?"

Jacob stomped to the other desk and plunked down hard. "Fine."

"Well, then, let's open our readers and begin with reading a story." Reagan picked up her book and cracked it open.

"Shouldn't we pray first?" Joseph's sweet face held no challenge, just inquiry.

Reagan tensed with embarrassment. "Of course." Jewish boys would most certainly pray first. How thoughtless. "Shall we bow our heads?"

The two complied, and she began. "Lord Je—"

She paused and glanced at the boys who stared at her with wide, horrified eyes. "Excuse me. Let's begin again." What had Mr. Bernheim prayed? Her mind raced to remember. She cleared her throat and tried again.

"Blessed are You, Lord our God, Ruler of the universe, who helps our minds to learn. Amen."

When she opened her eyes, Joseph had his hand raised, his body wiggling with excitement. Reagan acknowledged him.

"Can I please read from the Torah first?"

Oh my! The Torah? She looked around for what might appear to be a Torah but found nothing. She shrugged her shoulders. "I don't seem to have one here. Perhaps we'll ask your aunt for one and begin tomorrow's lesson with it?"

The boys complied, so she had them turn to their lesson. "Let's open to lesson twenty-five and see how we do. Who would like to start?" Joseph's eagerness contrasted blatantly with Jacob's reticence. Was that fear she saw in his dark eyes as he glanced at her, then promptly put his head down? "All right, Joseph. You may begin."

Once Joseph flawlessly read a few pages, she bid Jacob to take up where his brother left off. When he did, one simple page told her that the boy could barely read. Reagan's heart constricted as he struggled over nearly every word.

A large ship passed by the island just then, so Reagan rose and pointed to the left. "Look, boys! Where do you think that ship is headed?"

Jacob smacked his reader closed and hopped out of his seat as if a bee had stung him. "Downriver! To the ocean."

Reagan patted his shoulder. "Well done, Jacob! You're a clever lad." The boy beamed under her compliment. "And do you know what lies upriver?"

"Of course." He grinned triumphantly. "Lake Ontario."

"Excellent. I see you're very skilled with geography."

For several minutes, the boys chatted about being sailors and traveling around the world. Reagan loved their enthusiasm, but she needed to refocus them on their studies.

"All right, children. The ship has passed, so let's sit back down and turn our attention to writing."

After several moans and groans, the two were back in their seats. Reagan handed them each a sheet of paper and a pencil. "I'd like you to write a story about the frog you met the other day."

She gave them a few ideas, and the boys set to writing. Joseph's printing was nearly perfect, but Jacob's was squiggly and untidy with many misspelled words. Reagan's heart ached for the poor boy. No wonder he overcompensated outside the classroom.

Soon the breeze shifted, and the room became unbearably hot. Beads of sweat ran down the boys' faces as well as hers. "Shall we have our arithmetic lesson outside?"

In unison, the twins cried, "Yes!" They scooted from their desks and headed for the door. Reagan intercepted them, pencils and paper in hand.

"Stop! We are still in school and in your aunt's home. You will follow me, quietly. Is that understood?" She had to maintain discipline and decorum—or she would fail.

Jacob and Joseph nodded, so Reagan led them down the stairs and outside. On the veranda, she stopped and turned to the two. "You may run to the gazebo and wait for me there."

"All right! I'll beat you, baby!" Jacob challenged Joseph, and before he even said, "go," he was running toward the shore.

~ ~ ~

Daniel paused in pruning the surrounding hydrangea bushes when Reagan's slender form appeared on the veranda. "Top of the morning to you, my bonnie lass!"

Reagan sucked in a breath and threw her hand up to her chest, wide-eyed. "I didn't see you there, sir." A nervous giggle punctuated her surprise.

Daniel chuckled. "I didn't mean to scare you." He reached out to help her down the stairs, but she picked up her skirts and descended on her own.

"We were just going to the gazebo for our math lesson."

"May I join you? I need a break from this incessant sun. It's already hot." Did that sound too eager? A shiver ran down his spine even as sweat trickled down his temples. He wiped it away.

Reagan indicated her welcome, and he fell in step with her. "So, Miss Reagan, teacher of Casa Blanca, how's it going?"

She rewarded his words with a gentle smile and dancing eyes. "Fine. Though I don't have a Torah in the classroom, and apparently, that's an expectation."

"Oh, I have two! Let me fetch one for you, and I'll meet you at the gazebo." Without waiting for her to respond, he took off in a sprint, fetched the Torah, and returned ridiculously eager at the thought of giving her a gift.

Reagan quirked a brow at his quick return. "Why do you have two of them? Are you Jewish?"

He shrugged and handed the book to her. "My father and grandfather were."

She nodded and addressed the boys, who were busy counting the stones, one boy on each side of the gazebo. "Jacob. Joseph. Come and see what Mr. Daniel brought for you." The two ran to her side, but disappointment flashed on their small faces. "Tell him *thank you*. God's word is always a gift."

The twins murmured a *thank you* and returned to counting, while Reagan glanced at Daniel. "I, too, thank you for the book." She caressed the leather cover, which warmed his heart.

"Awww ... now I forgot where I left off!" Jacob stomped his foot. "Now I gotta start all over!"

Daniel lowered his voice. "What are they doing?"

Reagan gave that familiar, endearing giggle again. "This is their arithmetic lesson. They're counting the stones, one on each side. Then they'll add them together and divide them by two. It's an easy but active arithmetic lesson. I want to see what they know."

Daniel winked. "Clever."

Reagan bit her bottom lip before answering. "I adhere to Dewey's philosophy of education. Education should be a place for children to learn how to live, not just to fill their heads with facts. It's meant to help the student realize his full potential, how he's gifted, and not just be trained like a dog." Her eyes shone as she spoke. She really was a teacher at heart.

Daniel sighed. "How progressive. I fear the New York City Jewish elite might not agree with such a modern view."

Alarm filled Reagan's face, and it flushed a most becoming pink. "Will the Bernheims disagree with my methods? Dear me!"

He touched her forearm to calm her fears. "I'm sure it is fine as long as you don't counter Jewish traditions."

"But I don't know what they are. How will I know?" Reagan's high-pitched questions betrayed her insecurity.

"Do we count the pillars and the outside, too, Miss Reagan?" Judging by his eager tone and expression, Jacob seemed to be enjoying his task.

Reagan shook her head. "Not today. Just finish from the inside ledge, down. We'll count the rest another time."

The boys finished counting and handed their papers to Reagan. Once they added them together and divided the answer by two, she affirmed each of them. "It's time for some exercise. Let's take a walk along the shore, shall we?" Reagan gathered their papers and pencils and put them in the satchel she carried.

"Can we play hide-and-seek? Please, Miss Reagan?" Joseph stuck out his bottom lip, pleading with her.

"All right. But stray only as far as I can see you two." As they dashed off, Reagan rolled her eyes before

94

turning to Daniel. "However will I manage them? Bundles of unbridled energy, they are."

"Agreed. But you're doing just fine, lass." Daniel gently took her arm, puncturing the silence that fell with a bold inquiry. "I'd love to hear a little about your family, miss."

Reagan gulped, her fine features troubled. Had he tread on sensitive soil with his simple bid for information? "I grew up in Brooklyn and was the eldest of four girls. I used to be the apple of Papa's eye. In the summertime, he'd take my sisters and me for shaved ice after church on Sundays while Mama prepared dinner. We'd laugh, and he'd tell jokes and tease us for having dessert before dinner. Mama never agreed with that tradition, but he said it was a necessary evil to keep four girls in line."

Daniel chuckled and let her continue, though he didn't miss the fact that she said she *used to be* the apple of her father's eye.

She seemed to read his thoughts, or perhaps, the puzzled expression he couldn't quite conceal. "Papa hasn't been right in the head since the buggy accident where he and Mama and my little sister were hurt. We hoped the trouble with his head would be temporary and he'd heal from it. But now he's always angry and mean. Before I came here, he told me not to come home ever again if I fail at this folly."

Daniel touched her arm gently. "I'm so sorry. And what of your mama and siblings?"

She blinked back tears. "My three sisters are all younger and quite the close threesome." She paused, swallowing hard. Her bottom lip quivered. "Mama and I have always clashed. She even told me Papa liked me more than her and she hated me for it."

"We all have troubles, but family troubles are the worst, I think. I shall pray for you." He rubbed her hand, trying to console her as a shiver rolled through her, but it didn't seem to work.

She shook her head. "God has been silent since the accident. I've asked Jesus to heal Papa, but He doesn't answer." She blinked and stared at him for several moments as if struggling to form a question. "Forgive me. Are you—are you Jewish or Christian?"

Daniel shrugged, contemplating how to answer. "Well, now, that's a rather complicated question. My mother, God rest her soul, was Irish and a Christian. She got sick and went to heaven when I was but ten. My father was Jewish, so he always said I'm Jewish. Still, he rarely practiced his faith except on holy days. Mama's faith was strong and deep. When Father was away, she'd read me stories of Jesus and His disciples, and I found them fascinating. So … you needn't fear misspeaking around me. In fact, I'd like to know more … much more … about you."

Reagan's eyes sparkled as she nodded her pleasure.

"You did not!" Jacob's voice resounded in the distance.

"Did too!" Joseph countered. Then the two began wrestling on a rocky outcropping, Jacob throwing Joseph to the ground and jumping on him.

"Oh no!" Reagan plucked up her skirts and ran to the boys.

Daniel followed, passing her, beating her to the scene, and lifting Jacob off his brother like a dog from a cat. "That's enough, boys." He scolded the two, holding their arms to keep them away from each other.

Reagan stuck her hands on her hips, narrowing her eyes. "I'm disappointed in you both. I allowed you to play hide-and-seek, not roughhouse like a couple of hoodlums. It's time for science. Joseph, you go over and draw the day lilies. Jacob, you may draw hydrangea bushes over there." She handed each of them paper and a pencil and motioned to Jacob in the opposite direction from where she'd sent his brother. "After luncheon, we'll label their parts." She folded her arms, glaring at the boys until they trudged over to the flowers and began to draw.

She turned to Daniel. "That'll occupy them for a while."

Daniel chuckled and touched her forearm. "You're really good with them." Why did he always want to touch her? Be near her? He cupped her elbow, leaning in. "I'd better get back to work. You three distract me far too often these days." He winked, not letting go of her arm as Etta rounded the hedge and glared at them.

*Blathers! Not again.*

The lady's maid's eyebrows shot up. "What are you two doing? Seems mighty scandalous, I dare say." She glared at Reagan, ignoring Daniel. For the moment. "Are you not supposed to be attending to those rascals, miss? Shirking your duties to flirt with the boatman? Highly inappropriate for the servant of a fine Jewish family. But then, that's what comes from hiring a *Gentile*. Perhaps the missus should be informed … as soon as she recovers from her headache, that is."

The boys had stopped their drawing and stared at Etta, while Reagan's face had gone white. Daniel stepped forward. "That's ridiculous, miss. The boys are on an assignment from their governess, and I—"

"You were what, Daniel?" Etta sauntered up, a mixture of disdain and amusement staining her smirk. "Surely, you are not under her command too."

He stepped back, his muscles tensing. "I was merely bidding Miss Kennedy good day. And now, I'll do the same to you." Annoyance burning his insides, he took a few steps before pivoting back to face Etta. "There's an Irish saying, 'Who keeps his tongue keeps friends.' You'd do well to heed it, as there is nothing here to report."

~ ~ ~

Reagan sighed as she settled at the dining table between the twins and placed her napkin in her lap. What a morning! The memory of Etta's blatant threats and her possessive manner with Daniel still plagued her. She was glad she'd taken that walk with the boys to calm her nerves before luncheon.

Jacob pointed to a metal panel in the far corner of the room. "What's that, Aunt Mary? That thing with those funny pictures?"

Mrs. Bernheim grinned. "That's a Japanese screen that shows an Oriental fable. I can't recall what it's about, but perhaps you can ask your uncle when he returns. But enough of that. Let's bless our food." She prayed and began the meal. "So what have you three been up to today?"

Jacob stabbed a piece of chicken with his fork. "We went for a walk and saw the twin cottages. But they're not twins at all."

Mrs. Bernheim agreed. "That's true, but they were built at the same time and in a similar fashion, so the name stuck."

Joseph looked at his brother. "We're twins and we don't look alike."

The missus nodded as she set her fork down. "God creates each person unique. Even twins." She picked up her teacup. "Did you know that the owners of one of the twin cottages, the Strausses, are your great-aunt and -uncle?"

Jacob shook his head. "No. Never met them. Will we meet them this summer?"

"They're very busy people and only come here a few times each summer rather than staying the whole season, so we rarely see them." Mrs. Bernheim paused, her shoulders slumping. Then she addressed Reagan. "I fear we may not see him at all this summer. Nathan Strauss accompanied his brother, Isador, and his wife, Ida, to visit Palestine earlier this year. Uncle Nathan returned early, but Isador and Ida died on the *Titanic* in April. So sad."

Stifling a gasp, Reagan patted her lips with her napkin. "I remember hearing about that famous ship going down in the icy-cold water. Such a tragic accident."

Jacob turned to his aunt. "I'm glad Papa and Mamma weren't on it. They took a ship to Europe, you know."

Mrs. Bernheim leaned over and squeezed Jacob's hand. "Yes, but we got a telegram telling us they are safely there, remember?"

"I remember," Jacob admitted.

Mrs. Bernheim continued to enlighten Reagan, warming her with the way she addressed her as though they were equals. "While Mr. Strauss was in Palestine, he established a domestic science school for girls, a health bureau, and a free public kitchen. He even funded the Nathan and Lina Strauss Health Centers in Jerusalem and Tel Aviv. Most interesting of all, Uncle Nathan believed that God spared him, so he is giving two-thirds of his fortune to help Palestine. An amazing man, to be sure."

"And he's our uncle?" Jacob's eyebrows shot up.

"He is." Mrs. Bernheim winked. "We are a part of a special family, boys."

Reagan agreed. "That you are."

Later, while the boys composed letters to their parents, Reagan penned one of her own. She wrote to her family, sharing stories about the boys and the island and teaching, assuring them of how well she was faring, how much she enjoyed being a governess. She glanced at her two charges and grinned. Well, most of the time. She wouldn't mention the other times.

## Chapter 5

Reagan had gone up to the house to get some milk and muffins for the boys while they quietly played marbles on the pumphouse roof. Just two steps higher than the lawn, while the rest of the building resembled a cellar jutting out into the river, the roof was safe, at least for *most* children.

But when the boys' words carried on the breeze, something in their tones made Reagan freeze on the kitchen porch, straining to hear. What were they up to? Surely, they couldn't have found mischief so quickly.

"Come on, JoeJoe. All ya gotta do is smack it really hard with this oar." Jacob's plea was clear and unmistakable as he handed Joseph an oar.

What was the boy going to hit? A tree branch?

Joseph tentatively took the oar, shaking his head. "You do it." He thrust the wooden implement back toward his brother, who promptly folded his arms.

Jacob's eyes narrowed and his jaw jutted out. "I won at marbles, so you gotta do what I say."

When she realized what he was about to swat, Reagan set the tray down and ran as fast as she could to intercept their folly. "Joseph. Stop!"

But it was too late.

Joseph swung the oar toward a beehive hanging on a nearby tree limb, smacking it full on, sending it to the ground mere feet from his boots. Hundreds—maybe thousands—of angry bees swarmed from the hive!

Joseph dropped the oar and ran as fast as his legs could take him. Jacob did, too, outpacing his smaller, weaker brother. Joseph screamed for help, but before Reagan could get to him, he paused, huffing and holding his side. By then, a dozen bees hovered around him, dive-bombing, swooping, and stinging him as he swatted them furiously.

Reagan grabbed his hand, pulling him toward the house as she swatted at the bees, getting stung in the process. When they reached the kitchen door, they hurried in and slammed the door, a few bees joining them, causing quite a ruckus with the kitchen maids.

Mrs. Rosenstein hurried to care for Joseph and Reagan. She set Joseph upon the counter and applied plasters of cool, moist baking soda to soothe the stings. Then she tended Reagan. When all was said and done, Joseph had four stings, Reagan just two.

Reagan pulled Joseph close, ignoring her own pain, trying to comfort the teary, traumatized boy. Jacob was nowhere to be seen, and right now, she didn't care. "Are you all right?"

"It hurts. Why did Jacob make me do that?"

Reagan shrugged. "The Scripture says that foolishness is bound up in the heart of a child, but the rod of correction shall drive it far from him."

"Mama and Papa don't believe in spanking us," Joseph whimpered.

Reagan ignored that information, kissed his forehead, and rubbed his back. "I'm so sorry you got stung."

He snuggled up to her and wrapped his arm around hers. "I like you, Miss Reagan. A lot."

"And I, you. Shall we go and find your brother?"

Joseph nodded and hopped down from the counter, and Reagan thanked Mrs. Rosenstein. Joseph did too.

Reagan and Joseph found Jacob in his room in obvious remorse. His eyes were red, and his lips quivered as he volunteered a heartfelt "sorry" to both of them.

Grace. Perhaps Jacob just needed a little grace to change his ways.

After the noontime dinner, which they ate alone, Reagan allowed the boys to run to the tiny beach past the gazebo, towels in hand. Perhaps the cool St. Lawrence River would soothe hurting hearts and bodies.

The boys hiked up their britches and waded in the water as Reagan stood nearby pondering the day before. Daniel's protecting, caring hand on hers as she dared to bare her heart. He would likely make a good father and would train up his children well. But what about the sparks of anger she'd seen?

Suddenly, pebbles flew overhead, past her and the boys, plopping like hailstones on the river beyond. She turned around to see Daniel with that boyish grin of his, shrugging his shoulders and raising opened palms to the heavens.

"Hey, what's that about?" Joseph laughed as he spoke.

"Just checking to see if you're alive. You were standing too still to be boys." Daniel winked as he strolled up to join Reagan. "What were you looking at?"

Jacob grinned. "A baby eel keeps swimming around our legs."

"Ewww! There are eels in there?" Reagan pointed at the river.

Daniel smirked. "Just a few, and they're harmless."

Jacob tried to playfully splash the two, not even coming close to them but pulling her from her fears. "Can we swim, Miss Reagan? Please?"

"You may. But no deeper than your shoulders. Understood?" She tilted her head and, plopping her hands on her hips, waited for a reply. She even tapped her foot to emphasize her required promise.

The boys glanced at each other and turned back to her. Together, they chimed, "Yes, ma'am," and promptly dove underwater.

Reagan giggled, shaking her head. "Those two. What a morning! Bee stings and all."

"I heard about that, but it seems as though they're finding their footing with you, lass." Daniel gave her a little shoulder-bump, just for fun. She bumped him back.

"And I with them." She paused and looked at his handsome face as he watched the boys play. His joy was evident. "Do you want to join them, Daniel?"

A deep, rumbling laugh betrayed him, but he shook his head. "Not today. I need to work on the yacht motor this afternoon, but I wanted to say hello before I get all greasy and dirty. Still ... shall we sit a while? You might need more than one pair of eyes on those tadpoles."

Reagan giggled, glad to have reinforcements, and sat on the gazebo railing as Daniel joined her. Dare she ask what she'd wondered half the night? "So ... I shared my family story. Will you do the same?"

Daniel scanned her face until she felt a blush warm her cheeks. "I just knew you were going to interrogate me."

"You don't have to. I'm just curious, is all." Reagan folded her hands in her lap.

"Thank you," Daniel said. "But I don't mind. I, too, know a bit about wanting a parent's approval and never getting it. I was never enough in my father's eyes."

The pain and sadness on his face caused her pulse to speed up. She turned to him and, without thinking, said, "You're more than enough in my eyes."

Brows flying up, Daniel blinked at her.

Sucking in a breath, Reagan backpedaled as her heart dashed into hiding. "Sorry. I misspoke."

"Did you?"

Daniel stared at her until she shook her head, embarrassed by her truthful revelation. But when his sadness dissipated like a desert mirage, she relaxed.

"Thank you for that." Daniel patted her hand. "As I already mentioned, my mother was an Irish Protestant. Like the Marx family, my father a Jewish immigrant from Germany. My parents met on the ship and fell head over heels for each other. When Papa married Mama outside the faith, he became dead to my grandparents. I never knew them, nor did we speak of faith because of that. A

Jew marrying a Gentile is taboo, as I'm sure you know. And a child of such a union is a pariah. I am that pariah." He sighed, gazing at the clouds.

Reagan shook her head. "Neither of us may ever know the full affection and love of an affirming parent, but perhaps we can learn to see ourselves as God sees us."

"According to our faith, God sees me as a pariah. How is that comforting?" The bitterness in his words felt like a slap to her face.

"But that's not true. God loves all His children, and even though my faith has faltered of late, I know He loves me and sees each one of us as precious in His sight. The Bible says so."

"The Bible? Mama cherished hers. I'd find her secretly reading it when Papa was away." He paused and his tone softened. "Sometimes, she even read me passages that spoke of God's love. But when she died, I couldn't understand how a loving God could take my mother from me. And Papa? He became very bitter, and when he found her Bible in her unmentionables drawer, he shook it in my face and slapped my arm with it. Hard. He told me that it was all a lie, a deception made up to steal our Jewish heritage and cause us to burn in hell. Then he threw it in the fire." He rubbed his arm at the memory.

"I'm so sorry, Daniel." She paused, measuring her words. "I understand being mad at God. I'm still struggling to understand why my father has become so cruel. But He must have a purpose for everything, right?"

"Help! Jacob is missing!" Joseph's panicked cry caused them to jump up and dart to the shore.

The three of them split up to look for him. She yelled and hollered and scanned the horizon. Daniel jumped into the river, clothes and all, diving under the water to see if he could find him.

But no Jacob.

Guilt twisted Reagan's heart. If only she hadn't gotten so involved in talking with Daniel, this wouldn't be happening. Reagan lifted her hands to the heavens and cried, "God, help us!"

A flash of something entered the far periphery of her vision.

Jacob? That freckle-faced imp had been hiding behind a tree just off the beach's edge. Thank the Lord he was safe, but how could he engage in yet another form of rebellion mere hours after the bee incident? Reagan's blood began to boil until steam practically spewed out in her words. "Come here at once, young man! Now!"

Alarm struck his eyes as he sheepishly and slowly shuffled to her. Daniel popped out of the water and hurried to her, trailing river water, following close behind Joseph.

"You. Sit." She pointed at Jacob, then at the sand near her feet. Daniel's ire was palpable. So was Joseph's. The three of them just stared at Jacob as if he were a goose ready for the slaughter.

He was. At least with her words. "You, young man, know better than to pull such a prank. We've talked about your pranks over and over. You shall not go swimming for the rest of this week. Not a toe in the water. Not a fishing pole either. You scared us half to death! That was beyond naughty." She let out a huff and folded her arm to punctuate her words. "That was *bad*!"

Jacob folded his arms, too—in stubborn defiance.

"It was just a joke."

Now it was Daniel's turn to rail. "That is no joke. Pretending you've drowned? Never, ever, ever do that again, boy!" He paused and softened his tone, turning to Joseph. "Nor you."

Joseph shook his head furiously, his voice quivering. "I'd never, ever do that, Mr. Daniel."

Daniel nodded. "I know." He turned to Reagan. "I'll walk you back to Casa Blanca. I need to get to work, but I shall make sure this one gets back to the house safe and sound." He bent down and yanked Jacob up by his arm, shaking him. "Never do that again."

Jacob said nothing, and neither did she. They simply followed a very angry Daniel—still holding Jacob by the collar—up to the house.

~ ~ ~

Daniel still shook with rage long after Reagan and the boys disappeared into the kitchen. Foolishness, indeed! His father had raged at him every time he'd played a prank or did something childish.

His anger scared him. Would he beat his children as his father had done? Dear God! He hoped not. Yet inside, he felt the way his father had acted when he'd taken the strap or a stick or even the fire poker to him. No! He would never hit a child, even if he had to remain a bachelor all his life.

But still, visions of Reagan filled his head, his dreams of late. What might it be like to have such a wife? He pondered the idea as he worked on the motor, all through dinner, even until the stars began to pop out that night. He just had to shake those thoughts away, so he decided to take a walk around the perimeter of the island.

Then he saw Reagan, alone, standing on the veranda, gazing at the heavens.

What could it hurt to talk with her? After all, she was just a friend. The only real friend he'd had in a long, long time.

Daniel sauntered up the steps. "Good evening. The lads in bed?"

Reagan let out a deep sigh. "Finally. They've been more than a handful today."

A warm breeze kissed their cheeks and sent a loose strand of Reagan's hair dancing. His fingers twitched to brush it back, but he fisted his hands instead. Fireflies twinkled around her as if highlighting her presence.

"Isn't this evening glorious? Makes all the trials of the day float away. When I was on Dark Island, I often meandered along the shore just to take in its beauty. Somehow, water always gives me a sense of calm and peace." Reagan gifted him with her gentle smile. "See how the moonlight dances on the waves and plays with the light? I never tire of it."

"I admit that I haven't taken the time to notice of late, an error I must correct presently."

She pointed to the sky. "And aren't the stars a bower of beauty, twinkling so brightly tonight? It feels as though God Himself is sharing pinpricks of heaven with us."

Daniel followed her finger. "The stars are often this bright out here on the islands. The closer you are to people and their artificial light, the less majestic they seem to be. As a boy, I used to enjoy lying on the lawn and watching them for hours. I had hoped to see a falling star or a comet, but I'd often fall asleep out here."

Reagan sighed wistfully. "Sounds like a dreamy place to grow up."

"Yes. Well." He didn't want to talk about his lonely childhood. "Want to see my favorite spot?"

"Please." Reagan's excitement thrilled him to his toes.

Daniel took her hand and led her up the two steps to the top of the pumphouse, noticing that her tiny hand seemed to fit perfectly in his. "This area is sometimes used as an outdoor bandstand, a place for an orchestra and dancing when the Bernheims host parties. There's something about being smack-dab in the middle of this space that makes the heavens extra special." He took her in his arms to waltz, raising a challenging eyebrow. "Shall we?"

Tentatively, Reagan took his hand. "You may be disappointed. I'm not an accomplished dancer."

"No matter. It's the atmosphere and the company that make it enchanting." Playfully, he swung her around and dipped her. He felt her pulse speed up, as did his, and heat from her hand warmed his entire being.

Then he tapped out a one-two-three-four and began to hum "Lovely Lucerne," swirling around the pumphouse roof as if he wore tails and she a lovely ballgown that would accentuate her tiny hourglass figure.

"You're priceless, Reagan," Daniel said in a husky voice, the reality of his deepening feelings sending shivers of joy up his spine.

Reagan sucked in a breath and leaned into him ever so slightly.

Crickets chirped. The river lapped at the shore. Fireflies twinkled around them, creating a most magical moment. When he finished the song, he dipped her deeply, letting out a chuckle of delight. Then, pulling her to her feet, he cleared his throat, snapping into his more formal self.

"Do you know that this electric pump below our feet draws the water up to the water tower to provide pressure for the house? It's quite an amazing invention."

Reagan furrowed her brow, as if confused at his question. "No, I ..."

"Daniel? Are you out there? I hear your voice. Where are you?"

Etta. Again?

Daniel grabbed Reagan's hand and whispered close to her ear. "Hurry. Let's hide." Without waiting for her to respond, he pulled her to a corner of the bandstand, and the two tucked behind a pillar. He put his forefinger to his lips.

They waited until his legs ached from squatting and until they were sure Etta had gone on her way. Finally, they stood, laughing like two sneaky children at their victory.

"There you are, you … you Gentile vixen!" Etta stepped out from behind a tree and thrust an accusatory finger at Reagan. "You'll not steal the best of our Jewish men like so many Gentiles have done over the years. You'll not have him, ever, and you had best stay away from him. Do you hear me? Or the Bernheims will hear of it, and you'll be out on your ear." Her voice quivered, full of vehemence.

Who was she to say such things? Though it may be a wee bit improper to dance in the moonlight with a young, female employee, it should be none of Etta's concern. His face flamed at the thought.

At his error. Awareness exploded in his mind. If he considered himself a confirmed bachelor, he had no business playing with Reagan's heart.

A slice of guilt cut deep.

Yet... was he to be a pawn for someone like Etta to play with? To manipulate?

He looked at Reagan, wilted and fearful. The poor lass could lose her position and bring shame on her head. She could lose her dream.

Perhaps Etta was right. Perhaps he should steer clear of this lovely Gentile. Was Reagan the forbidden fruit that Genesis talked about? The one thing that would endanger his work, his community, his future?

And endanger her.

What was he thinking? He was just as his father always said he was.

A disgrace to the family.

## Chapter 6

Reagan balanced the tray as she stepped out on the blue-and-white veranda and glanced at the boys, quietly playing jacks, for once. A yawn escaped her lips. It had been a disquieting night of vacillating between dreams of Daniel and the magical moments in his arms and fretting over Etta's threats of ruining her. Why was the woman so against her, anyway?

And then, with the return of Mr. Bernheim to the island, it seemed all the more dangerous to even talk to Daniel. Yet she needed to, to beg him to keep his distance even as she wanted to be near him.

She pushed away the thoughts and turned to the beauty before her. If she lived to be a hundred years, she'd never get tired of seeing the river and the tiny islands dotting it! And this part of the river was even more enchanting than downriver where Dark Island was.

She surveyed Casa Blanca's veranda. The sky-blue ceiling reminded her of the heavens above, and the plethora of wicker furniture seemed perfect for the enormous wrap-around porch. When the boys stopped playing jacks and looked up at her as if to say, "what next?" she had an idea.

She set the tray of milk and cookies on the wicker coffee table. "Boys, let's count the pieces of furniture—silently—and see if you come up with the same amount. Then we'll have a snack."

Jacob and Joseph scurried around the porch, touching each piece of furniture, mouthing the numbers. She counted them quickly too.

Jacob returned first and whispered in her ear. "Thirty-two!"

Joseph joined them and answered, "Thirty-three."

Reagan glanced from one boy to the other. "Seems we have different numbers. Shall we recount?"

Off they went and returned with the same numbers. Reagan shrugged her shoulders and addressed Joseph. "I'm sorry, lad, but I counted thirty-two as well."

Joseph pointed at a wicker shelf hanging on the wall. "Did you count that? It's wicker."

Jacob shook his head. "That's not furniture."

"Is too!"

"Is not!"

Reagan pulled them apart before a scuffle ensued. "I see both of your points. Though it doesn't sit on the ground, that shelf could be viewed as a piece of furniture, so you both win! Well done."

She handed each of the boys a glass of milk and set a plate of cookies between them. "There are two cookies for each of you. Be sure to share."

Reagan took a sip of her water and set down her glass. "Do you know, boys, that until recently, many babies and children often died from drinking milk?"

Joseph scrunched up his nose, pushing his milk away. "Why? Milk is good for us. Mama always said so. So did Nanny."

Reagan nodded. "Yes, it is, if it's pasteurized and not raw swill milk. And I'm sure your milk is always pasteurized."

Joseph pulled his glass back toward him and took a bite of a cookie. Jacob gobbled and guzzled, thoroughly engrossed in his snack.

"Last night I read a newspaper article about your great-uncle, Mr. Strauss, the one your aunt told you about. Do you know that he helped to keep children from dying? He believed in Louis Pasteur's discovery of pasteurizing milk, so he built a plant to sterilize milk bottles and kill the bacteria in raw milk. At his own expense, he established dozens of care centers that gave good, healthy milk, food, and coal to the poor of New York City. He even built shelters for the homeless."

"That was very kind of him," said Joseph.

Jacob finally joined in. "What's swill milk?"

"It was poor quality milk that brewers and distillers sold, and it was often contaminated with typhoid, diphtheria, and cholera. Mr. Strauss had three children,

132

and two of them died. He was convinced that the milk killed them."

Mr. Bernheim slammed open the screen door through which he must've been listening for some time. "Enough! This conversation is not appropriate for young boys. Do you want to scare them to death?"

Reagan stood and curtsied low. "I beg your pardon, sir. I was only trying to speak the praises of your uncle and teach them a little history. And science."

Mrs. Bernheim slipped onto the veranda behind her husband. "Yes, well. Though Mr. Strauss is a great philanthropist, please refrain from sharing information that might frighten the twins."

Reagan swallowed hard. "Certainly, ma'am. Sir. I beg your pardon." She bent low and dipped her head in contrition, her heart thudding.

*Isn't knowledge power, and isn't that what a teacher is supposed to impart? How do I find that balance?*

"Very well. Carry on." Mr. Bernheim tossed her a wary look and gave a half-hearted nod to Jacob and Joseph. "Boys." Without waiting for them to answer, he turned and disappeared into the great room. With her lips pressed together, his wife followed.

The boys stared at her with wide eyes and furrowed brows. Jacob seemed to shake it off faster than Joseph. Like always. "Can we go and see the gargoyles down by the river, Miss Reagan?"

She quirked a brow. "You may, but remember you cannot get into the water this week, and you mustn't climb on the statues."

His shoulders slumped, but he recovered quickly. "I remember. Come, JoeJoe. Beatcha to the lion!" Off he scampered, while Joseph rose slowly and slipped his hand into hers.

"I don't like the gargoyles. They're scary." He lowered his chin and shuffled as they followed Jacob.

"They're just big, stone statues, dear one. They're supposed to ward off evil spirits, though I'm sure that's just a fairytale."

"I don't like fairytales either. Or witches. Or mean people. Is Uncle a mean person?" He looked up to her, waiting for an answer.

"No. But I suspect he's just not used to having little boys about. He means well." Reagan hoped that answer would suffice.

"That's what Mama says about Papa." With that, Joseph let go of her hand and joined his brother where four ugly gargoyles overlooked the main shipping channel. Two had wings. Two had long, protruding tongues, painted red. All four had red eyes and mouths. She agreed with Joseph. They were scary.

She descended the steps that led under a huge rock arch where a giant granite lion stood watch above. She joined the boys in a recessed lawn, a moat-like grassy area encircled by rock walls from the gazebo almost to the pumphouse. The gargoyles were bigger than she realized, much larger than Daniel. Vines covered the base of the statues and, thankfully, kept the boys from touching them. But as Jacob tried to climb up on the rock wall, Reagan stopped him.

"No, Jacob. You can run and play in the grassy area and climb on the island-side wall but not on the riverside. It's quite a drop off into the river and simply too dangerous. Is that clear, boys?"

The twins complied, and a lively game of tag began. Meanwhile, Reagan marveled at the rock-work and beauty around her. Perhaps she'd sketch the artistically chiseled lion and gargoyles one day. She'd enjoyed teaching the boys a bit about drawing, and Jacob seemed quite proficient. At least, more than in handwriting.

A dozen or more banjo-shaped, white, wooden windows ran the length of the moat. Upon bending down for closer inspection, she found that electric lights lay hidden behind the grillwork. How marvelous the island must look from the river at night, all lit up and twinkling in the darkness!

She turned to check on the boys, but there was no sign of them. "Oh heavens!" She grumbled, Mr. Bernheim's scolding and the constant threat of her failure ever upon her. "Boys. Where are you?"

She hurried toward the hidden area of the moat where it turned toward the river side of the gazebo. No boys. Those two could disappear faster than hummingbirds could flutter.

"They're over here." Daniel's voice called from the direction of the boathouse. She climbed the rocky knoll that rose between the gazebo and boathouse. When she got to them, the boys offered a "sorry" even before she could speak.

Jacob was unusually contrite. "We were just checking to see what Mr. Daniel was hammering, Miss Reagan. Honest Abe."

Daniel tossed her a look that melted her worries, so she let it pass. This time. "All right. But next time, please tell me when you're leaving my sight. I don't want to lose you."

"You can't lose us on an island." Jacob grinned.

"Oh, but I fear I could." Reagan winked.

"Might you like to take a boat ride before dinner? We could cross the channel and view Castle Rest on Pullman Island if you'd like. I need to test the engine I've been working on." Daniel nearly begged Reagan with his dark, penetrating gaze.

Reagan scanned the area to see if Etta might be around. Perhaps it would be all right and give her a chance to speak with him about keeping his distance. "I suppose it would be fine, as long as we're back in time to clean up before dinner at one-o'clock. Would you enjoy that, boys?"

Joseph and Jacob clapped their hands and jumped up and down. "Yes. Please."

Again, she looked for Etta's nosy presence.

"Something bothering you, lass?" Daniel held out his hand for her to board the skiff. The boys were already sitting quietly, wiggling with excitement.

She took his hand, his touch sending warm waves of excitement through her. What was it about this man that thrilled her to her toes?

Pulling back her hand, she sat, stilling her racing heart. She had to warn him to stay away. She just had to.

~ ~ ~

Daniel eased the skiff away from the dock, pondering the nervous energy that emanated from Reagan's being. What was bothering her and why?

"Penny for your thoughts, my lovely lass?" Daniel hoped to get an answer easily.

No such luck. A deep, uncomfortable silence lay thick between them.

Reagan cleared her throat and leaned toward him so the boys couldn't hear. "You must stay away from me, Daniel. I ... I don't want any impropriety. I am here to serve as a governess, to get a good recommendation, to become an accomplished teacher. Do you understand, sir?"

Sir? The chill in the air felt like a blustery January day. Goosebumps popped out on his forearms, even in the warm sunshine. Why the change in her?

Her eyelashes fluttered, her tone softening in explanation. "I feel my future is in danger at every turn. There's Mr. Bernheim. And then there's Et——."

Daniel nodded, the reality looming large before him. "Yes, Etta. Beware of her, for she has the mistress's ear and her trust."

Reagan glanced at the boys who were preoccupied with the boats passing by. "But why? I cannot fathom it."

"Apparently, she's a fine seamstress and excels in doing the missus's hair. I overheard the accolades of Mrs. Bernheim several times."

"Can everyone not see past her skills and pretty face?"

"I can. Just you mind that." Daniel winked, but instead of a smile, he received a narrow-eyed flash of fear.

"Still. Please keep your distance. For my sake … and yours." The pleading in her expression tugged at his heart. But something about her drew him to her like a key to a magnet.

He turned to steer the boat across the main channel in front of an oncoming freighter. How could he agree to stay away from the only person who had warmed his heart since his mama left him for heaven?

"That ship is going to hit us, Mr. Daniel!" Joseph pointed at the vessel, a hundred or more yards away.

"Steady, lad. We're safe. We'll pass in front of it before it gets here."

Daniel shook off the distance he felt from Reagan by donning his tourist persona. "We're coming upon Pullman Island, home of the railroad tycoon, George Pullman and family. Did you know, boys, that President Ulysses S. Grant visited the island back in 1872? His visit made the islands famous. Thanks to him, the Thousand Islands are now full of the rich and famous and their spectacular homes, castles, and cottages."

Reagan's silvery eyes twinkled with interest. "The Bournes spoke of the presidential event, but I didn't realize it took place so close to where I'm now working. To think the president saw what I now see." Her entire face lit up. Then she turned to the boys. "Did you know President Grant was a famous general in the Civil War?"

The two shook their heads. Apparently, she needed to teach a bit of history to these boys.

Daniel slowed the boat and pointed to the immense stone castle on the island. "Castle Rest was built in 1888, so the president didn't see this magnificent place. There was a more modest cottage then, but thousands came to a reception and met him. Some other Civil War generals were also there."

"I wish we could go into the castle." Joseph motioned toward Castle Rest. "Are there knights guarding it, do you think?"

Reagan giggled, tickling Daniel's emotions. "No. Knights lived many centuries ago. Not today."

Daniel slowly eased the boat around to the opposite side of the island and pointed to a large land mass with cottages sprinkled along its shoreline. "That's Wellesley Island, in Canada, the second largest island in the Thousand Islands." Then he motioned to an island next to Pullman. "And this is Nobby Island."

Jacob pointed. "These islands are so close. I could swim from one to the other."

Reagan nodded. "You probably could, young man. I believe you're quite an accomplished swimmer from what I've seen."

Jacob beamed at the compliment, but Daniel shook his head. "No swimming here or along the main channel, young man. The currents are way too strong and would pull you into grave danger. Besides, the many boats make it doubly unsafe."

Jacob's eyebrows furrowed, and both boys looked over the side as if to view the currents. Reagan leaned over and trailed her fingers through the water, creating ripples that glistened in the sunshine. "Heed Daniel's warning, boys. This river is full of beauty, mystery, and danger."

Suddenly, a large yacht steered into the channel, threatening to overtake their small skiff. "Hold on lads.

Miss." The three took hold of their benches as Daniel steered toward the Pullman Island docks. Joseph stood to step onto the dock, but Daniel wiggled a finger at him. "Sit down. You can't step onto other people's property without being invited, lad. These are private islands."

"I'm sorry. I didn't know." Joseph looked like he might cry.

"It's all right, laddie." Daniel winked at him, attempting to ease his fears. Once the yacht passed, he headed back across the channel to Cherry Island.

~ ~ ~

Reagan murmured a thank you as she avoided Daniel's outstretched hand and stepped on the dock. The boys scurried ahead of her toward Casa Blanca and the dinner that awaited them.

Hurrying back to the house, she scolded herself for being so cold and unkind. It wasn't her nature, but what else could she do to ward off his apparent interest?

She entered the twin's room, bid them to wash, and helped comb their hair. "Let's hurry to dinner, boys. We mustn't be late. And remember ... be quiet little gentlemen."

The two complied perfectly, slipping into their seats and murmuring greetings to their aunt and uncle. Mr. and Mrs. Bernheim greeted the twins and glanced at Reagan before bowing their heads.

"Blessed are You, Lord our God, Ruler of the universe, who creates varieties of nourishment." Mr. Bernheim finished his prayer, and the lot of them murmured, "Amen."

After silent eating for a few moments, Mr. Bernheim set down his fork. "Tonight begins Shabbat, boys. You shall follow it well, wearing your yarmulke from a few minutes before sundown tonight until three stars appear in tomorrow night's sky." He turned to Reagan. "We will keep a quiet respite in prayer and in the Torah. They shall not play, nor partake of childish foolishness. To that end, since the entire staff joins us for Shabbat, so you may. Tomorrow, Jacob and Joseph will spend the day with me, as their male guardian, in prayer and in reading the Torah. You may have the day off."

"Of course, sir." She glanced at Jacob and Joseph, who looked rather disappointed.

"Very good." He paused before continuing. "Boys, your governess is not required tomorrow, so you must be on your best behavior. I'll have no foolishness or you'll answer to me. Is that understood?"

The twins murmured, "yes," their eyes wide with uncertainty.

What would these boys do all day? What would she do?

That evening, while the boys sat at the table with their aunt and uncle, Reagan was sent to the servants' table. Etta eyed her with disdain, creating an altogether uncomfortable evening.

Even so, she soon found that the Shabbat dinner was rather interesting. The housekeeper lit candles and prayed in another language. It was a beautiful, strange custom, with reverence and awe on the faces of everyone, including Daniel—and Etta. Despite her enjoyment, Reagan felt rather an outsider.

After prayers were said, two braided loaves of bread called *challah* were broken, and joyful banter ensued. Everyone said, "Shabbat, Shalom," to each other, and Reagan did, too, guessing it was a special greeting.

Daniel was also at the servants' table, and she felt his eyes upon her more than once. Yet, with all her willpower, she refrained from returning his gaze, knowing that Etta might use it against her, either now or in the future. By the end of the drawn-out and strange evening, Reagan was thoroughly exhausted, ready to rejoin her charges and their sweet acceptance of her.

## Chapter 7

Reagan's day off proved refreshing as well as inspiring, though she found she missed the playful banter of the boys. For the first time in a long time, she'd plunged into reading the tiny Bible that Miss Marjorie had given her the summer before. Though she had rarely looked at it until now, she wanted to know more about the twins' namesakes, Jacob and Joseph.

She found their names and read from Genesis 37 all the way through to the end of the book. Her family had never gone to church regularly, and although Sundays with the Bournes were days of spiritual reflection, she'd not heard much of these two biblical characters nor wondered about them.

Jacob, it seemed, was the patriarch of the family, and Joseph was his favorite of twelve sons. She wondered at the story of Joseph and his colorful coat, his dreams, his trials. She also found it interesting to read of the brothers' jealousy, their treachery, their deception. And she prayed for her two charges to become men of honor, truth, and kindness. Like Daniel.

Never had she met a man quite like Daniel. Why would God allow a woman like Etta to come between the friendship that had blossomed between her and Daniel? Was God punishing her for her negligence? Her failures?

Reagan sighed, wishing she understood the God who seemed so far away. Did He still love her, or was

Daniel right? Was she, too, a pariah to Him? The thought made her blood run cold in her veins. No! It couldn't be.

She returned to reading about Joseph's ups and downs, especially the false accusations of Potiphar's wife that had him thrown into prison. Could Etta be a Potiphar's wife? Could Etta's lies imprison Daniel? Her?

Reagan snapped the Bible closed and left her hot, stuffy room to get some fresh air. She wound her way through the hallway toward the servants' stairs, past the twins' empty room.

An entire day with Mr. Bernheim. How were they faring? Such energetic boys must be itching for freedom. She tossed up a prayer for the boys' peace as she descended the stairs to the kitchen. The servants' area and kitchen were empty and quiet. Shabbat was quite a peculiar custom, albeit rather refreshing—not unlike the Bournes'

Sunday Sabbath. One day of seven to rest, just like the Creator of the universe had done.

Instead of walking toward the gazebo or boathouse, Reagan decided to meander in the direction of the twin cottages in hopes of avoiding Daniel or anyone else, for that matter. She found a rocky outcropping that would serve as a nice perch and sat down. She opened the Bible but startled when a woman's laugh sounded from the bushes behind her.

Etta? Wasn't she supposed to be with her mistress?

"You have no business fraternizing with that Gentile, Daniel. No proper Jewish man would be caught with the likes of her. I'm a better choice. A thousand times better than *her*!"

"Let me pass, miss. I'll not be party to your shenanigans. And for your information, I have already decided that I shall remain a bachelor and never marry. Not you. Not anyone. So be about finding another man."

Reagan's stomach churned at his confession. Why, just last night she'd dreamt of Daniel, no doubt because of the way he'd encouraged her interest. Today he said he wished to remain a bachelor?

Etta snorted, mocking Daniel's confession. "You'll marry. I know you. And it might as well be me. We're of the same lot and would get along splendidly, if you'd just accept that fact. I could be the woman you'll desire forever." Her voice lowered suggestively on the last, and Reagan's fingers fluttered to her lips.

"Not you. Especially not you!" Daniel's voice rose to a higher pitch than Reagan had ever heard. Angrier than she'd ever heard.

Etta nearly screeched like a hawk after its prey. "You'll regret this! You will, Daniel."

Reagan strained to hear what came next, but the conversation seemed at an end. A shuffling sound, a flutter of hummingbird wings, the piercing call of seagulls, a boat or two on the river. But no voices.

Yet she felt storm clouds gather. Not the kind that bring rain, but the more insidious kind that bring troubles.

One of the kitchen maids appeared, rather flustered and fidgety. "Excuse me, miss, but you're needed in the house." She beckoned Reagan with an impatient wave. "Missus said to hurry."

Closing her Bible with a sigh, Reagan followed the maid back to the kitchen. Mrs. Rosenstein met them at the door, grabbed Reagan's hand, and pulled her into the butler's pantry. "It appears Jacob has misbehaved once too often and incurred the wrath of Mr. Bernheim. He's washed his hands of the boy, sent both of them to their room, and recalled you to your post at once. I'm sorry you shan't have the time off as you expected. But duty calls."

Reagan curtsied. "I was actually missing them just now."

The missus quirked her head and let out a most unladylike cackle. "Missing those two imps? You're a curious one. Be about it, then."

Reagan hurried up the stairs and found the boys lying on their beds, yarmulkes flung beside them. She knocked at the open door, stepped inside, and gently closed it. "What happened that you are imprisoned in your room?"

Joseph glanced at Jacob, who had his back to them. "He got fidgety like he always does and knocked over the inkpot onto Uncle's important papers. Uncle was furious and hit him. Then he sent us both away and said he didn't want to see us until we could behave like good

Jewish boys. Jacob didn't mean to do it, Miss Reagan. Truly."

Reagan went over to Jacob and rubbed his back. The boy scooted away for a moment but then accepted her affection. "He hates me. Everybody does."

"I don't. I love you, Jacob." She gathered him into her warm embrace, and the child whimpered like a baby. Joseph joined them and patted his brother on the shoulder.

"I love you, too, Jacob." Joseph swiped a tear away and tried to cheer his sibling up with a riddle. "Why were Adam and Eve sugar planters? Can you guess, Jacob?"

Jacob squinched up his face and shook his head.

"Because he had to raise Cain! Sugar cane. Get it?"

The three spurted with laughter, dispelling the gloomy moment.

"Good one, Joseph!" She simpered and further attempted to change the mood. "Shall we go outside and get some exercise?"

"We can't. Uncle said we can only read the Torah and pray for our wicked souls." Joseph rolled his eyes. "That's boring."

Reagan corrected them gently. "Now, now. God's word is never boring. Why, just today I was reading about Joseph and his colorful coat. Shall we go to my room where there might be a cooler breeze and read the story? Then you can picture it in your imagination and draw it while I read. How does that sound?"

The boys reluctantly agreed and followed Reagan to her room. Indeed, a cool breeze blew in the open side windows, making for a rather pleasant atmosphere. "Why don't you climb up onto my bed, just this once, since it isn't school?"

The boys scampered onto the bed, and she gave them a box of Crayola crayons and sheets of paper and began to read the story of Joseph and his brothers.

~ ~ ~

Daniel followed the setting sun that scattered orange, red, and gold gems on the rippling river around him. He steered the skiff out to the main channel, determined to release some pent-up frustration and get away from the island, if only for a little while.

Blathers! How was he going to keep Etta from acting on her vicious threats? Nearly every time he encountered that woman, his temper got the best of him, which only caused her to threaten retaliation. She was not one to lose a fight, of that he was sure.

What was he going to do? Though he feared she might cause him difficulties, he worried that Reagan might be the brunt of her evil schemes instead. He couldn't let that happen.

Truth was, if he were to ever marry, Reagan would be the kind of woman he'd want to spend the rest of his life with. Nae! He could never trust himself with such a tender soul. His temper might get the better of him, and then what?

As the sky darkened, he returned to the island just as concerned as when he'd left it. No resolution for his anger, Etta's warnings, his future. Or Reagan.

Remembering that he needed to gather his laundry from the laundry house, Daniel lit his oil lamp and headed that way. Entering the small building, the smell of lye soap accosted his nose. He quickly gathered his small pile of clothes and retreated to the fresh air.

"Good evening, sir." Reagan sat on the servants' porch, rocking in the breeze. Her formal salutation seemed cold, guarded.

Daniel nodded. "Good evening, miss. Care for a stroll on this fine evening?" Innocent enough. Just two friends on a walk.

Reagan glanced around like a frightened rabbit, but then straightened. "All right. I do need to stretch my legs."

"Mind if we drop my things at the boathouse?"

Reagan agreed, and he blew out his lamp. The starlight guided them as the two strolled in silence, but not for long. "How was your Shabbat?"

How could he answer that without disclosing Etta's threats? "Fine."

"I found it refreshing, although poor Jacob fell into disfavor with Mr. Bernheim, and I had to occupy them the rest of the day. 'Tis hard, indeed, to keep young boys quiet and happy while confined to one room. By bedtime, they were ready to end their upsetting day in slumber."

"I admit that, as a wee boy, I found the winter days indoors more than I could endure. Yet, if I were to become a solicitor, that would be my lot in life."

Reagan stopped and quirked her head. "A solicitor? Is that what you aspire to?"

"Aye. But I fear it is but a distant dream. My mother's brother was a famous solicitor in Ireland, and she told me many stories of him saving innocent people from their doom. Ever since, I've wanted to help others as he did." Giving a wry smile, Daniel shrugged.

Reagan's eyes twinkled in the moonlight. "So why are you here and not in the courtroom?"

Her question was innocent enough, her tone not judgmental, but indignation rose within him, nonetheless.

Why not, indeed? "Money, of course. What else keeps able bodies such as we to the mundane tasks we hold?" His tone was bitter and a bit harsh, and he cringed at the sound of it.

Reagan took a tiny step back and sucked in her breath. "I'm sorry, Daniel. I didn't mean to pry."

Clutching his bundle of clothing against himself under one arm, Daniel scooped up her hand in his. "Nae. I'm sorry. My temper too often gets the better of me when I feel cornered, criticized, or condemned."

Reagan squeezed his fingers, sending a lightning bolt of awareness through him. "I meant none of those. You are a clever chap and should aspire to such a place of service. This is the twentieth century, for heaven's sake. Should we settle for what we are supposed to be rather than what we are meant to be? That's why my father, Mr. Bernheim, and likely many others, think it folly for me to teach rather than be a lady's maid." She wrinkled her nose and frowned.

Daniel dropped her hand and waved his toward the boathouse, bidding her to walk. When they got there, he set his lantern and the pile on the steps leading to his apartment. "They'll be fine there, unless a varmint comes a-visiting."

Reagan giggled, shattering the gloom of their conversation. It was time to turn to brighter topics.

"You have quite a modern philosophy of life, and you're a talented teacher. I've seen you turn those leprechauns from their folly time and time again. However did you learn to do that?"

Reagan bobbed her head. "Miss Marjorie Bourne inspired me to be a modern woman, and though I wasn't schooled in the art, I read several books on education from the Bournes' library and took them to heart."

"I, too, have been reading many law books, and I apprentice under Solicitor Thomas Goodwin of Alex Bay in the winter. He's getting on in years, and I hope to take on his practice one day. Yet I'm needed here in the summer and receive a fine wage for my work, so I can't yet give this up. Finishing my apprenticeship is taking so much longer than I had hoped, and though I've drawn up contracts and wills, learning law is daunting. Though Mr. Goodwin has been more than patient with me, I fear I may be an old man before I can finally practice." Daniel's stomach churned at his admission.

"Slow and steady, chap. You have the will, and I trust you'll achieve your dream in time." Reagan's cheerful encouragement somehow irritated him.

"What do you know? I'm twenty-five and should be established by now! I should be settled in my life, not wallowing here on this island in a life of service."

166

Reagan's eyes flashed with alarm, and she stepped away. "I'd better get back to the house and retire. Goodnight, sir." The sadness in her voice grieved him, her use of the word *sir* accentuating the emotional distance he'd created between them.

*Why do I always hurt the ones I care for?*

He shook his head, for he'd vowed never to be like his father. Yet he seemed to become like him more and more each day. He tried to spit out the bitter taste in his mouth, but it didn't do any good. In resignation of his failure, he retreated to his apartment.

~ ~ ~

Reagan swallowed back the tears that threatened. Every time she found herself drawn to Daniel, lowering her own walls, he raised his quills and shot one or two her way. Those barbs hurt. Yet when he was nice, her heart raced at the thought of being near him. He was handsome, kind, clever. And he had aspirations beyond this island. Desires to help other people, to serve others.

Still, she had to keep her distance. She'd pleaded with him to stay away. Yet, time and time again, there they were, walking and talking and enjoying time together—until his temper or Etta's presence crumbled magical moments into dust. Was that God's way of telling her she was on the wrong path? That it was best to stick to her resolution to keep him at arm's length?

Sleep came slowly as she tried to sort out the unsortable. To understand why she was so attracted to this man. To comprehend why Etta was so hateful. After an irksome night of tossing and turning, she awoke grumpy and tired.

"Miss Reagan. Are you coming to breakfast? I'm hungry." Jacob's muddled voice carried through the door, accentuated by a gentle tap.

Goodness! She'd overslept.

"Coming. Wait in your room for just a few moments." She hurried and dressed, pulled her hair back into a chignon, and gathered the twins from their room. "Thank you for waiting, boys. I appreciate it."

Joseph grinned as he stared at her face. "Miss Reagan, you have sleepy lines all over your face."

Reagan rubbed her cheeks as they grew warm. "Goodness, I expect I must have slept on my tummy. Do you?"

Jacob chuckled as they descended the stairs to the dining room. "Joseph sleeps on his back and snores."

"Do not. He's fibbing again." Joseph stuck his tongue out at his brother.

Reagan placed her finger to her lips. "Quiet, boys. Act like gentlemen. Remember?"

The two rolled their eyes but complied. They straightened, took the handrail, and walked down the rest of the stairs like little soldiers. Quietly, they slipped into their chairs, laid their napkins in their laps, and folded their hands.

"Good morning, boys," Mrs. Bernheim greeted them cheerfully, then dipped her chin her way. "Miss Reagan."

All three glanced at Mr. Bernheim's empty chair. The missus answered the mystery. "Your uncle left early this morning on a business trip. He'll be back by week's end. Let's see if we can stay out of mischief when he returns, shall we?" Under a kind and understanding smile, the boys relaxed.

Mrs. Bernheim prayed, and they began to eat in silence. But then she set down her teacup. "I regret the accident yesterday, Jacob, and the resulting slap. Please excuse my husband. He doesn't have children around him very often."

Jacob waved a hand. "Awww…, it's okay, Auntie. I get in trouble all the time."

Everyone gushed with laughter, and the conversation turned into happy banter. Reagan's heart grew light for the first time in a long time. Perhaps the winds of tribulation might blow over the island after all.

## Chapter 8

Reagan sat next to Jacob as she watched Mrs. Bernheim give Joseph his afternoon piano lesson, pleased to hear impeccable scales, "Twinkle, Twinkle," and "Happy Birthday." But now the child struggled to play "*Fur Elise.*"

"You can do this, Joseph. The black notes and some of the jumps between notes are farther than those in 'Bach's Prelude in C Major,' but you're a capable pianist. Let's try again." The missus's kind encouragement made Joseph straighten his back, ready to tackle the piece.

Reagan bent to whisper in Jacob's ear. "You already know this piece, don't you, my clever chap?"

Jacob wiggled in his seat. "Yes, but it's good to hear Joseph so I don't make the same mistakes."

*So that's why he sits so still at the piano lesson every afternoon.*

Just then, Mr. Bernheim swept into the music room with a large bouquet of roses. "Happy anniversary, Mrs. Bernheim!"

The missus stopped Joseph from playing the piano and stood, rosy pink cheeks coloring her surprised face. "Welcome home, husband. I thought you weren't getting here until evening."

"I caught the early train." He handed her the bouquet. She buried her nose in the blossoms, took an audible sniff, and promptly sneezed.

"*Gesundheit.*" He planted a kiss on her cheek, and the boys chortled. Reagan turned away to afford them a private moment.

Mr. Bernheim took his wife's hand but didn't move from the doorway. He tossed them a greeting. "Hello, boys. Miss Reagan."

For the first time ever, Reagan witnessed a wide smile on the man's face. His eyes twinkled and his mustache rose. The grin on his finely molded features made him more handsome than she'd ever seen him.

"I have another surprise for you, wife." Dramatically, he stepped aside and waved his arm as if to announce a famous guest. A tall, balding, bespeckled man appeared in the doorway. His grey, receding hairline ran from ear to ear, and his mustache just touched the corners of his lips.

"Happy thirteenth anniversary, daughter!" The cigar in his hand likely caused his scratchy voice.

Mrs. Bernheim blinked twice. Then she hurried to him and threw her arms around him. "Father! What a pleasant surprise!"

"That's what I hoped. Your husband's plan worked." He didn't reciprocate her hug but stiffly nodded before addressing Mr. Bernheim. "Well done, boy." He then eyed the twins, looking down at them as if they were a dog or a cat. "And who might these be?"

Jacob and Joseph stood and slowly made their way to him but didn't seem to know him. Reagan stood where she was, uncomfortable being party to such family intimacies. Should she slip out or wait for instructions?

"I'm Jacob, and this is my younger twin brother, Joseph." Jacob reluctantly took the man's outstretched hand and Joseph followed. "Our mama is his sister." He glanced at Mr. Bernheim.

"Good to meet you." The man didn't acknowledge him, and his rigid, authoritarian manner alarmed her. Even the flower in his lapel didn't soften his demeanor.

Mrs. Bernheim cast wary eyes on her. "Miss Reagan, please take the twins outside for some fresh air while we entertain Mr. Marx. And let us not be disturbed."

Reagan curtsied. "Certainly, missus. Come, boys. This way." She waved a hand at the far door leading to the west side of the veranda, and the two scurried to join her. Outside, both boys blew out a breath.

"That cigar was stinky." Joseph pinched his nose and frowned.

Jacob grimaced. "He looks mean. Better stay clear of him."

"Now, boys. Let's be charitable. After all, he is your great-uncle." Reagan winked.

"What's so great about him, anyway? He looks like an old goat." Jacob took his usual challenge position, arms folded, toe-tapping, chin down.

"Enough, or you'll be sitting instead of running and playing." Reagan shook a finger at him. Time to engage them in positive play. "All right, young men. Let's play hide-and-seek. I'll be the seeker, but mind you, no yelling, wrestling, or fighting."

Jacob and Joseph looked at each other and then at her. In unison, they hollered, "Yes!"

"Let's keep our voices down. Noise carries on the breeze here, remember? I'll count to one hundred, and you go hide. If I find you, you have to run to this point"—she patted the porch pillar—"and touch this before I touch you. Any questions?"

The twins shook their heads, and they began looking for a hiding place.

"All right. Ready. Set. Go!" Reagan turned around and started counting slowly, hoping to have a few moments of peace and quiet.

Why did a pleasant woman such as Mrs. Bernheim have such ambitious, authoritarian, stoic men in her life? Surely, she found it most distasteful.

Oh dear! She'd forgotten to count. She picked up at seventy and spoke the next few numbers aloud.

Would Daniel become a strict man like them or a tender man like Mr. Bourne? She hoped the latter. Yet no matter. He was nothing but a friend and never would be more. But still …

"One hundred! Here I come, ready or not!" Reagan scanned her surroundings and saw no movement, no sign of the boys. She started searching around the powerhouse, gazebo, and moat area, but neither Jacob nor Joseph were to be found. Then she headed toward the icehouse and laundry house, but they weren't there either. Between the two small buildings, she saw a door at the back of the laundry marked, *Tool Shed.*

Perhaps they hid there?

Opening the door, she stepped into the darkness, her eyes adjusting slowly as she looked around. She hurried to the far side to peek in a large cupboard. As she did, from behind her, a sound of footsteps drew her attention toward the door where Jacob gingerly exited. Before she had a chance to reach him, he slammed the door closed! "Got you. Try and catch me now!" The boy's muffled voice taunted her.

Making her way to the door in the dark, she tried to open it but couldn't. "Jacob. Let me out of here at once!" No sound came from the other side, so she wiggled the doorknob and repeated her demand. Nothing. Not a sound. She banged on the door and yelled for help, but it was several minutes before someone finally came.

"Just a moment."

Daniel? Here to rescue her, again, from the wiles of those rascals. In truth, what would she do without him this summer?

The door opened, and light flooded in, blinding her for a moment. The annoyance on his face irritated her. "What in heaven's name are you doing in here?"

Reagan's frustration spilled over. "Looking for a hammer to hit you over the head?"

"Let me guess. Jacob." It wasn't a question. He groaned. "Still, this is partly my fault. The door latch tends to stick. Need to fix it."

Reagan wiped the sweat from her brow and smoothed her hair. She pushed up her sleeves and stepped into the fresh air. "It's hot in there." And she now very much regretted her generous offer to play the game. She looked around. "Where can those boys be?"

Daniel wiggled his finger for her to follow. "I may be able to solve your dilemma. Come with me."

"What? Another tryst?" Etta had stepped out on the back porch, hands on her hips, a glower on her face. "In broad daylight? Well, I never!"

Reagan scowled at her. *For heaven's sake! Can she not mind her own business?*

"We haven't time for your shenanigans, miss! We have two missing boys at present." Daniel's voice was taut. He didn't wait for Etta to answer, didn't even look at her, so Reagan followed him in silence.

Daniel went straight to the pumphouse and entered into a room under the roof on which they had danced. Spiderwebs laced the ceiling. A huge pump took

182

up about half the room, groaning like a sleeping giant awakening from its slumber. Several stored pieces of old furniture and equipment prevented her from spotting the boys. But she could hear one suck in a breath and another titter. There, to their left, two pairs of eyes peeked out from behind an old chaise.

Daniel tossed her a look that said, "Give it to them good."

She narrowed her eyes and put her hands on her hips. In as stern a voice as she could produce, she said, "Jacob. Joseph. Come here at once!" She thrust a finger their way, then pointed at the space between herself and Daniel.

The boys slowly obeyed, Jacob biting his bottom lip and trying not to laugh, while Joseph quivered as if seeing a ghost. "Told ya not to do that, Jake." Joseph's whisper reverberated in the room.

When the boys reached them, Daniel promptly took hold of Jacob's ear and pulled him out into the sunshine, with Reagan and Joseph following close behind. Once they ascended the steps to the grassy knoll, Daniel gave Jacob a good shake and growled, "What were you thinking? I should take a willow branch to your backside, I should!" Daniel's face was as red as the paint on the passing freighter, and Reagan feared he might haul off and smack the boy.

She stepped to his side and kept her voice even, gentle. "Jacob, my disappointment brings me much sorrow. I thought we'd overcome your naughty pranks, but this one is the worst. Why would you do such a thing when we were having fun? I want us to enjoy our time together, but perhaps we should only do schoolwork."

"I'm sorry, Miss Reagan. I only wanted to get to the porch before you. I didn't know it would lock on you."

Jacob's remorse was palpable. "The rabbi says foolishness is bound up in my heart." He shrugged as if he were chained to the declaration.

"The rest of the text says that the rod of correction will drive it from you!" Daniel took a step toward the boy, but Joseph stepped in his way.

"He didn't mean to. Please, Mr. Daniel. Papa and Mama don't spank us. They forbid it." Joseph's voice trembled as he pleaded.

"Perhaps that's the problem." Daniel shook his head and waved an arm. "Oh, I wash my hands of you. But let it be known that if you hurt Miss Reagan in any way, I *will* tan your hide, parents' edict or no!" He stared down both boys, darting his narrowed eyes from one to another. Then his gaze turned to her.

"If either of these rascals causes you any more trouble, come to me, and I will deal with them.

Decisively." With that, he turned on his heel and huffed his way back toward the boathouse.

Reagan blinked as he stomped down the path. With a temper like that, could Daniel be trusted as a disciplinarian? All romantic notions aside, it gave one something to think about.

~ ~ ~

When Daniel returned to the boathouse, he splashed water on his face, trying to cool his anger. Jacob. Etta. Mr. Marx. What more could he endure?

Just hours ago, the boat ride to fetch Mr. Marx had incited his current foul mood. Mr. Bernheim had spent the entire trip discussing "the unconventional choice of tutors for good Jewish boys." He railed about Reagan, calling her an uneducated, undisciplined, incapable Gentile woman, spitting out the words as though they were gall on his tongue. He asked that Mr. Marx set his daughter straight and implore her to find a proper caregiver for his nephews.

Daniel let out a bitter laugh, mumbling to himself. "If anyone can teach those two about right and wrong, Reagan would be my choice, Gentile or not!"

Why did there have to be such prejudice between people? If they only knew her, they'd see she was a woman of faith and wisdom beyond her years. Mr. Luis Marx, a successful sugar and tobacco planter in Cuba, was known for his fine cigars. Though a mighty successful businessman, was his faith deeper, stronger, better than Reagan's? Was *his*?

Daniel shook his head. "Not mine." With this admission, he grabbed the sandpaper and began working out his frustration on the bottom of the small boat he'd been sanding for the past several days. He wrestled with the two sides of his faith journey for several hours, questioning his own Jewishness. How had it benefitted his father? Etta? Himself?

Etta claimed to be a good Jewish girl, but he saw nothing of character in her. Schemes. Plots. Threats. How he despised her!

Recalling an Irish proverb his mother had often said, he spoke it aloud, trying to set his sour thoughts aright. "May you never forget what is worth remembering, nor ever remember what is best forgotten." Laying down his tools, he plunked down on a nearby stool. "Lord God, help me to remember my mother's faith and forget my father's faults. And the things he did while calling it faith."

A tear slid down his face. Then another. Then another. Swiping them away, he struggled to regain composure, even though he was alone.

"Daniel? Are you here?" Reagan called from outside the boathouse, her voice strained.

"Coming!" Daniel wiped his face with his shirtsleeve and his hands on his pants, sucking in a deep breath before showing his face to her.

When he saw Reagan, fear surged in his blood. "What's wrong?"

Reagan's eyes were swollen, her shoulders sagging, her face downtrodden. "I've been banished from the cottage. Etta told tales about our relationship, and Mrs. Bernheim was furious. Said she didn't want to see me until her father left the island. Sent a kitchen maid to oversee the boys who are imprisoned in their room." With that, she threw her hands up to her face and wept.

"I'll skin that woman alive. I will! Tell tales, indeed! I have a few tales about Etta that would curl the hair on the missus's neck." Daniel fisted his hands and began pacing. He couldn't touch Reagan. Comfort her. He wanted to, but he shouldn't. Likely, that vixen would appear out of nowhere with a journal in her hands, ready to take down everything to incriminate them further.

"She wouldn't believe you. Etta has her hoodwinked, convinced I'm the wily one, and she's a saint. And don't be surprised if they come after you too."

He stopped and stared at her. "What did she say?"

"She told the missus we were having a tryst in the toolshed and have had several rendezvous of a scandalous nature. She told the missus I've neglected the twins time and again and that they are endangered by my presence. Mrs. Bernheim said she would deal with me after Mr. Marx is gone, and I am to take a room on the third-floor servants' quarters for the night! Oh, Daniel, what am I to do? I cannot fail at this position. I cannot!"

Suddenly, his mother's face came to mind, her council at such difficult times a vivid memory. After his father railed at him, falsely accused him, belittled him, or beat him, Mama always said the same thing. "Trust and pray that the God who sees all will bring truth to light. Eventually."

Throwing caution to the wind, Daniel took Reagan's hands in his and repeated his mother's counsel. But instead of his words calming the woman, she began to cry. Hard.

"That's what Papa would say, too, before the accident. But now he beats my mother, and I couldn't stop him. Seems I've failed her—and God. How can truth and justice come from such circumstances? I cannot fathom it."

Taking her into his arms, he held her tight as she wept on his shoulder.

How, indeed?

When her tears were finally spent, he gently pulled her from his embrace and kissed the top of her head, holding his lips there for several seconds. She drew in a soft breath. "Your father's deeds are not your fault, but we *shall* pray, Reagan. To the God who sees all and knows all. And I will ask that He answer soon."

## Chapter 9

Three days of isolation. Three nights of worry.

Putting herself in seclusion, Reagan stayed in her third-floor room praying for truth, for freedom. She saw no one, save an occasional kitchen maid who brought her meals.

Like a bird from her perch high atop Casa Blanca, she'd caught glimpses of the boys, heard them play, and seen a timid kitchen maid watch them. She listened to an entire day of rain pattering on the roof until she thought she'd go mad.

She'd also seen Daniel a few times, and once, caught Etta dramatically talking to him, shaking her finger and then stomping away. Early on the morning of July fourth, Mrs. Bernheim finally summoned her to a meeting.

Reagan descended the staircase to the second floor and softly knocked on the missus's bedchamber door. Beads of perspiration wet her brow and the palms of her hands, and she swiped them away.

"Come in and close the door, please." Mrs. Bernheim's voice was steady, not quivering mad like when they'd last spoken.

Reagan entered, taking a deep breath to calm her nerves.

The missus sat in a light-blue chaise. She set aside the book in her hand and waved for Reagan to come and take a seat in a hard, straight-back chair. Once seated, Reagan folded her hands in her lap as the missus began.

"Seems you have several of our islanders in your corner." She paused, eyeing her as if trying to read her. Reagan lowered her eyes to the morning sunshine flitting across the floor, trying to keep her emotions at bay. "I had a visit from Mr. Lovitz, Mrs. Rosenstein, two kitchen maids, one laundry maid, and both of the twins! I felt as though I was called to be judge and jury these past few days."

Reagan sucked in a breath. What had they said about her? Her eyes darted to the missus and then right back to the floor.

"Perhaps I condemned you prematurely after hearing tales from only one person. Upon learning of your banishment and the accusations leveled against you, the others, who came to me voluntarily, have refuted the claims of misconduct, negligence, and scandal. Mrs. Rosenstein even went so far as to plead your case and vouch for your character. In all my years, I've never heard such praise from that woman's mouth."

What should Reagan say to this information? Should she thank the missus? Agree? She had no idea, so she remained stoic and still but timidly raised her gaze to the missus.

"Therefore, I shall grant you clemency and return you to your position immediately." The missus tossed her an apologetic glance. "From what the maid tells me, the twins adore you and have moped about the island for most of these past few days pining for you to take your place again. They even cried themselves to sleep every night."

"I adore them, Mrs. Bernheim, and hope to make a difference in their lives, however small."

"Seems you already have. Now go and tend your charges with my apologies. I fear that kitchen maid won't last another day with them."

"Yes, ma'am. Thank you, ma'am." Reagan began to stand, but the missus held up a hand to stop her.

"A word of warning before you go."

Reagan eased herself back onto the chair and refolded her hands.

"Mr. Lovitz has admitted his interest in continuing a friendship with you and has vowed to maintain all social decorum. He assured me of your innocence in any of the prior accusations and pledged he would be a gentleman in every circumstance. I expect you to conduct yourself as a lady, a governess, and my employee at all times. Is that clear?"

Reagan nodded her head vigorously, her eyes pleading. "Of course, ma'am. I shall do my utmost to execute my duties honorably and faithfully."

"Very well, then. Let us put this entire nasty business behind us, shall we?" Mrs. Bernheim grabbed her book and opened it. "As today is a day of celebration, we will all attend the fireworks in the bay this evening. See to it the twins rest this afternoon so they can enjoy the events."

Reagan stood and curtsied. "I will, missus. Thank you for your forgiveness."

Mrs. Bernheim shook her head. "Apparently, there's nothing to forgive. Now go find the boys."

Reagan curtsied again and fled the room. Acquittal! "Thank you, merciful God!" Without waiting another moment, she hurried to the boys' room but found it empty. She scurried down the servants' stairs to the kitchen, where Mrs. Rosenstein was busy telling her staff of the day's events. When the housekeeper noticed Reagan, she motioned for her to wait.

"The family has given us all the night off to attend the Fourth of July festivities in the bay. Mr. Lovitz will shuttle us at seven o'clock sharp and return at ten p.m. Be on time for both—unless you want to stay on the island or be stuck in the bay for the night. Furthermore, the day's chores must be completed by five p.m., or you'll remain behind. Understood?"

A chorus of "Yes, ma'am" ensued, the grins of the staff showing their appreciation.

"Carry on, then." Mrs. Rosenstein turned to Reagan. "A word outside, please."

She curtsied and followed her to the back porch. Before Mrs. Rosenstein spoke, Reagan did. "Thank you for your word of support to the missus."

"I cannot abide false accusations, gossip, or innuendos. I have seen you with Mr. Lovitz and have never seen the behavior you were accused of. However, I have seen it among others in the past, and I simply won't tolerate it. I have vouched for you, so be careful not to disappoint me."

"Yes, ma'am! Thank you." Reagan curtsied again.

Mrs. Rosenstein touched her shoulder. "Very well. Go and find those rascals and return my maid to me." After waving toward the distance, the missus returned to the kitchen.

Mercy. Full and free. Merely minutes ago, she was a caged bird. Now free to fly, Reagan wanted to sprout wings and soar on the breeze. But with her feet firmly planted on the earth, she picked up her skirts and hastened to find her boys.

It didn't take long. There they were, pants hiked up, knee deep in the water where they'd experienced the frog episode, just past the gazebo. "Hello, boys. I'm back." Reagan's voice quivered with joy, excitement, and relief. She held out her arms to receive the river-soaked twins who hurried into her embrace with squeals of happiness. She didn't care that they splashed mud on her skirts or dampened her blouse.

"Oh, Miss Reagan. We've missed you so. We told Auntie we needed you." Joseph glanced at the maid.

"Thank you, miss. You may go." Reagan acknowledged the maid, who promptly fled their presence.

Jacob shook his head as he watched the girl leave. "She was so boring. Wouldn't let us do nothin' fun."

Reagan lifted his chin. "That's 'anything fun,' and let's be kind. Remember, she left her regular work to look after you."

Jacob squeezed her around the waist. "Yes, ma'am. I'm glad you're back. I'll be good. Promise."

Reagan giggled. "Don't make promises you can't keep, but do try, sweet boy." She hugged him back before letting go. "Now catch me up on all the news."

The three plunked down on the grass, and the boys began an animated tale of the past three days. Joseph started. "We had a whole day in our room when it rained. The maid wouldn't let us do nothing ... anything but draw and color and read. We even had to eat in the kitchen whilst Mr. Marx was here."

Jacob chimed in. "It was awful. Like Auntie and Uncle wanted to hide us or something. Do they not like us anymore?" With a frown and a pout, the boys implored her to answer.

Reagan reached out and took their hands and squeezed them. "They love you both, but sometimes older people get irritated by all the vivacity that oozes out of two active, noisy boys." She let go of their hands and started tickling them. The boys rolled onto their backs and whooped and wiggled as if they just had to expend some pent-up energy. Then they rolled away from her and down the small hill that led to the sandy area and then to the water. They rolled and rolled until they rolled right into the river.

As if they hadn't realized where they were going, both boys brimmed with glee, splashing and chasing each other with abandon. Reagan laughed, too, enjoying the joy-filled play, wishing she could join them.

"Oh, to be young again! Aye, miss." Daniel appeared by her side, startling her.

"Goodness! You gave me a fright." Reagan threw her hand to her chest to calm her thumping heart. "Good day, sir." She smiled wide, happy to see him.

"You've been set free, I see. Never prayed so hard in all my life. Spent some time in the Scriptures too. Glad you've been emancipated." Daniel's eyes were misty, kind, sad. "Your circumstances of late reminded me of an old Irish saying, 'As you slide down the banisters of life, may the splinters never point the wrong way.' I hope you didn't get many splinters over this incident."

Reagan giggled, contemplating this multi-faceted man before her. "Thank you, I think." She slipped her hand into the crook of his arm. "I heard you paid the missus a visit. Thank you for that too."

"Had to. Couldn't let an innocent lamb be led to the slaughter, now could I?" Daniel gave her a tender gaze.

"Come and join us, Mr. Daniel. It's fun!" Jacob attempted to splash them.

Reagan waved toward the river. "Go on, then. Join the fun."

Daniel pulled off his boots and socks, emptied his pockets of a handkerchief and a few screws, and dove into the water. He engaged the boys in a game of tag, stating they couldn't go deeper than their shoulders nor get out of the water.

Reagan's heart swelled with joy to see Daniel and the boys again. While he played water tag with the two leprechauns, Daniel frequently snatched glimpses of her and even winked once. She grew self-conscious until she had to pace back and forth, trying to decide how to handle the mixture of feelings she had for the man. How to keep proper distance? She had no idea.

Soon the three climbed out of the water and sat in the sunshine, winded but laughing. "I won the game of tag, Miss Reagan!" Jacob declared.

Reagan took his hand and squeezed it. "Did you, now? Congratulations. Perhaps I should declare you a muskie rather than a tadpole."

"What's a muskie?" Joseph looked to Daniel for the answer.

"A muskellunge is a prized sport fish here in the St. Lawrence River. It's quite narrow with a flat head." Daniel spread his arms as wide as he could, and since he neared six feet tall, that was a bit of a stretch. "They can get this long, but usually about as tall as you, Jacob, and could weigh almost seventy pounds."

Reagan joined in the conversation. "Mr. Bourne caught a huge one last summer. Their teeth are scary."

Daniel concurred. "Yes, but that's so they can eat other fish and not little boys."

Jacob wiggled. "I want to catch one someday."

Comfortable silence slipped between them for a few moments before Daniel faced her and swallowed hard, imploring Reagan with his dark, warm gaze. "Would you mind if I escort you and the boys to the bay tonight so we can enjoy the fireworks together?"

"Would it be appropriate? I fear scandal, Daniel."

Daniel shrugged. "I've already cleared it with the missus. Since Mr. Bernheim is here, she agreed I should escort the three of you to the bay and not have the twins about his feet."

Reagan let out a giggle. "Well, then, so be it."

~ ~ ~

As the stars twinkled above, Daniel asked Reagan and the boys to remain in the boat until the last of the staff disembarked onto the Otter Creek dock, then he addressed them. "I'd like to take you over to Casino Island. With the casino closed today, not many people will bother to go there, and the view of the festivities should be spectacular."

Reagan glanced at the twins. "Sound good, boys?" The two nodded in agreement, eyes wide with anticipation.

Daniel saluted them, like any good sea captain would, and earned laughter from all three. He followed the shoreline around a small peninsula until they came to Casino Island, about thrice the size of Angel Isle. He brought the boat onto shore where not more than a dozen people milled about.

Reagan took his hand to disembark, sending a shiver of excitement through him. "'This is lovely, Daniel. Thank you for bringing us here."

"You're welcome." Daniel bowed slightly before helping the twins out of the boat and grabbing the large basket she'd brought.

When they got to a grassy knoll that overlooked the main channel, Reagan spread a quilt, and the four of them sat. She opened the picnic basket and gave them each a glass of lemonade, several cookies, and set out a bowl of blueberries, raspberries, and cherries.

"Oh, yum! Thank you, Miss Reagan!" Joseph grabbed for the fruit, but Reagan held his hand back. "Let's use our manners. Only a small handful at a time. And remember to share. Daniel, why don't you go first?"

Daniel ever so slowly reached for the berries as two small boys licked their lips, waiting for their turn. "Don't you feed these two? Looks as though they're about to faint dead away from starvation."

"Naw ... we had dinner. We just love berries, Mr. Daniel." Joseph's seriousness made him chuckle, so Daniel handed the bowl to the boys.

The four nibbled on the treats and enjoyed the lemonade while waiting for the sun to fully set and the sky to darken. Chatting about past firework displays, Reagan admitted she'd only seen one. Joseph and Jacob gasped at her admission.

"We've seen plenty, Miss Reagan, and we're only eight." Joseph bit into a cherry and spat out the pit before continuing. "But we haven't seen them here. I hope they're as wonderful as the ones in New York City. One time we saw the Statue of Liberty light up with fireworks." Joseph turned his face to the sky as if his words would make them begin.

"I've seen them here every year, and they're wonderful, dancing a jig on the river like they do." Daniel grabbed Jacob's lemonade before it spilled. "Careful, laddie."

Soon the sun slid behind the horizon and stars began to twinkle. Jacob wiggled. "It won't be long now."

Reagan rubbed her thin arms. "It's getting chilly. I should've brought a wrap. Are you boys cold?"

Jacob and Joseph didn't look away from the sky, but Joseph waved a hand. "We're fine."

Throwing caution to the wind, Daniel tossed the quilt behind them over her shoulders, scooted close to her, and put an arm around her, rubbing hers. He was just keeping her warm—purely practical.

Before he could move away, Reagan laid her head against him, just for a moment. But in that moment, everything changed. His bachelor heart turned; his purpose sealed.

Suddenly, the fireworks lit up the sky, echoing his thoughts. Explosions of beautiful colors washed Reagan's awe-struck face with light. In the midst of flames and sparks, noise and smoke, they *ooh*ed and *ahh*ed, cheering and laughing like children at Christmas. The colorful, sparkling shapes continued as Daniel's heart soared.

Similar explosions warmed his heart. Thoughts of life with this woman. Prayers for her success. Dreams of the future he'd never before dreamed.

Reagan turned her sweet face up to his, surprise and pleasure mixed with … could it be desire? With all the self-control in him, he resisted the urge to kiss her as she voiced just what he was thinking. "This has been one of the best days of my life. Thank you for sharing this evening with me. I'll remember it forever."

Daniel gave her a tender squeeze and planted a kiss gently on the top of her head, lingering there a wee bit more than he probably should have. "I agree, my sweet. I agree."

But how? How could he court her on this tiny island without getting into trouble?

# Chapter 10

"Hurry, Miss Reagan. We can't be late for Shabbat dinner." Joseph plopped on his yarmulke and pulled her toward the door. "The sun has almost set, and Uncle is very strict about being on time."

Reagan prodded Jacob to join them. "Come, Jacob. Your aunt invited me to join you to help. I fear you two shall have to guide *me*."

"We will," Jacob said as he slipped his hand in hers. "I hope we'll have honey cakes for dessert." He licked his lips like he'd already tasted them.

"I hope so, too," Reagan agreed as they descended the stairs.

Entering the dining room, Reagan took a deep breath at its beauty. The table was set for royalty with the most beautiful crystal, lace, and silver. Two large candlesticks held white candles, yet unlit. The butler in his finest livery stood at attention.

Mr. and Mrs. Bernheim entered as Reagan and the twins settled into their seats, greeting her as they all took their places. This looked much more formal than the servants' Shabbat. How would she manage without being able to mimic the staff as she'd done before?

Mrs. Bernheim stood, lit the candles, and waved her hands over them three times, apparently saying a silent prayer. Reagan tried to relax in the solemn peacefulness that filled the room.

Then Mr. Bernheim stood, and Reagan peeked to see if she should fold her hands or what she was supposed to do. She followed the missus's lead when she simply bowed her head. He began, "Blessed are you, O Lord our God, King of the Universe, you are the author of peace …" He went on to talk about the holiness of the Sabbath, the candles driving out the darkness and lighting their way.

Everyone joined him with an "amen," and Reagan felt God's gentle presence fill the room as Mrs. Bernheim sat. Then, Mr. Bernheim surprised her by going over to the twins, laying his hands on the boys' heads, and praying for each of them before breaking into a song of blessing.

Reagan's eyes stung with tears, but she blinked them back. Never had she seen Mr. Bernheim so loving and tender. The boys sat unusually still and quiet as Mr. Bernheim returned to his seat.

"Blessed are you, O Lord our God, King of the Universe, who creates the fruit of the vine." Mr. Bernheim took a sip from a crystal goblet of wine and passed it to his wife. Mrs. Bernheim handed it to Jacob, who took a gulp and handed it to her. She took a sip and passed it to Joseph. He took a large swallow, then returned it his uncle. He leaned over to Reagan and whispered, "That was the *Kiddush*."

Next, the butler brought a bowl of water with a towel hung over his arm. From Mr. and Mrs. Bernheim, to Reagan, to the boys, each washed their hands and dried them. She supposed it meant they were to be clean, but she wasn't sure.

Mr. Bernheim prayed. "Blessed are you, O Lord our God, King of the Universe, who brings forth bread from the earth."

The missus repeated this prayer and so did Jacob. Was she to repeat the prayer too? She did, and Joseph followed.

Jacob whispered, "That was the *Hamotzi.*"

Two loaves of bread sat on the table, covered with intricately tatted cloths. Mrs. Bernheim ceremoniously removed both cloths, and each of them tore off a piece of the bread and ate in silence. How interesting to have only bread for dinner!

Yet just as she was thinking that, the butler set a large, silver bowl before them. He removed the cover and proceeded to ladle a golden chicken soup into bowls and place them before each of them.

"Oh, Auntie, *yoich* is my favorite!" Joseph yanked another hunk of bread from the loaf, and soon, both loaves were gone. Jacob slurped the soup, dribbling it down the front of his clean, white shirt. He plucked his napkin from his lap and began to frantically wipe it. "Sorry. I spilled."

Reagan patted his shoulder before dipping a corner of her napkin in her water and dabbing the stain until it could barely be seen. "Let's tuck your napkin here." She slipped it into his neckline as the missus gave her a discreet shake of her head. Reagan promptly pulled it out and laid it on his lap. She shrugged her shoulder and mouthed, "sorry" to the missus, who returned to eating.

Apparently, good Jewish boys didn't tuck their napkins.

When dinner was finished, the butler removed the bowls and set small plates before each of them. Jacob leaned in and whispered, "It's honey cake. I just know it."

Sure enough, the butler presented a golden bundt. He cut the cake and served it. Almonds and raisins made it a most delightful treat, and the missus allowed the boys to have a second piece.

Mr. Bernheim cleared his throat. "Jacob and Joseph, remember that tomorrow is a day of rest. No wild boy nonsense."

Joseph dabbed his lips, missing a bit of cake on his cheek. Reagan wiped it clean. "Yes, Uncle. But can we go outside, please?"

Jacob shifted in his seat. "Yes, Uncle. God wants us to admire His creation, and when I do, sometimes I even think of a prayer or two."

Mrs. Bernheim laughed into her napkin. She glanced at her husband, who clicked his tongue. "You may, but no foolishness." Then she turned to Reagan. "Mr. Lovitz has offered to take the three of you on a quiet boat ride, and we have agreed. But make sure the boys wear their yarmulkes and behave, Miss Kennedy."

Jacob and Joseph cheered, but Mr. Bernheim stopped them with a raised hand. "Enough. It is to be a quiet, reflective trip, not a wild Indian party."

The twins said in unison, "Yes, Uncle." The silently left the room, but their grins betrayed their excitement.

~ ~ ~

The next afternoon, Daniel readied the skiff for the boat trip. Perhaps he'd weave them through the Friendly Islands, around St. Elmo, and up to Heart Island so they could see the magnificent Boldt Castle. Surely, they'd enjoy that.

"We're here, Mr. Daniel!" Joseph's voice carried on the breeze, his excitement palpable.

"Welcome, boys. Miss Reagan. I trust we shall have a peaceful trip?" He eyed the boys warily and then chuckled.

221

"Yes, sir." Joseph slipped his hand into Reagan's.

Soon the four were settled into the skiff, and Daniel started the engine and steered the vessel out into the main channel.

"Why are we using the engine?" Reagan asked as she pushed wisps of hair away from her face.

"It's the Sabbath. Rowing is work." Daniel shrugged before turning to the boys. "Who kept the first Shabbat, boys?"

Jacob answered. "Moses!"

Joseph shook his head. "Nope. God did, to show us how."

"Very good. Shabbat is a sign of God's covenant with His people." Daniel steered the boat parallel to a steamer heading toward Lake Ontario. They turned in the opposite direction toward Alexandria Bay and then veered north, the hum of the engine and the warm sunshine refreshing. Daniel slowed the boat as he guided it between a large land mass and several small islands. "To our left is Wellesley Island. To our right are the Friendly Islands."

"May I request a favor?" Reagan bit her lip after asking.

"Anything."

"I'd like to understand Shabbat better. The prayers. The symbolism. It's so beautiful."

Joseph raised his hand as if he were in school. "I can tell you. Rabbi Richter said I excelled in learning the Torah and its ways."

Jacob bumped his brother. "I can help too. I'm not a dummy."

Reagan reached over and patted them both on their knees. "You're both clever chaps, and I'd be pleased to learn from both of you."

Daniel winked at her. "There's an Irish saying, 'Praise the young and they will flourish.' Carry on, then." He slowed the skiff to a crawl so he could hear the discussion.

Jacob shot his hand in the air. "Me first. The candles show us when God created light. The wine gives us joy."

"And we wash our hands before we lift them up to God," Joseph added.

Daniel interjected. "Very good. And what of the bread?"

"The *Challah*? It's braided like this." Joseph folded his arms over his middle. "When your arms are folded, you can't work, and the Shabbat is a day for resting."

"And there are two loaves 'cuz God gave a double portion of manna on Fridays, and the lacy covers are the

dew that the Israelites saw before the manna appeared."
Jacob grinned.

"Really? That's so amazing. Thank you." Reagan glanced at the boys before turning to Daniel. "We worship the Light of the World and the Bread of Life."

Daniel nodded, and they shared a special smile before he again prompted the twins. "And when we return home? What of the Sabbath evening?"

Joseph shrugged. "Oh, that. When the sun starts to set, we go to the table again and eat supper. But we have to finish before three stars come out. That's when the Sabbath is over."

"But tell her about *Havdalah*," Daniel prodded.

Jacob wiggled in his seat. "That starts the new week. I want to hold the spice box this week, okay, JoeJoe?"

Reagan's brow furrowed. "Spice box?"

"Sure, Jacob." Joseph patted his brother's shoulder before facing Reagan again. "The spice box is called the *Bessamen,* and it smells real good. That reminds us that life is good, and the twisted candles show us creation and redemption. I'll hold them tonight." His shoulders straightened as if it was an important honor.

"Goodness! Such beautiful ways to reflect God. Thank you, boys. I shall forever be grateful that you were the ones who enlightened me."

Jacob and Joseph grinned from ear to ear.

Daniel cleared his throat. "Not to take away from this wonderful lesson, but we are now passing Belle Island. The Peacock family built that beautiful, yellow Colonial Revival-style villa a few years ago."

"It's lovely with the green roof and wrap-around porch." Reagan's eyes twinkled, and he caught a glimpse of the silvery flecks in them.

"Just ahead is Imperial Island. The impressive stone mansion looks like it belongs in England with knights standing at attention, aye, laddies?"

"Does a king live there?" Jacob asked as they passed the fortress-like structure.

"No, the Pittsburgh industrialist, Gilbert Rafferty, lives there."

The four admired the structure in silence, but only for a moment. "We're now on our way to Heart Island." Daniel jerked his chin straight ahead to where another imposing castle came into view. "That's Boldt Castle."

"Are there knights and fair maidens in *that* castle?" Jacob swiped the air as though he brandished an invisible sword. "And might there be a dragon to slay?"

Reagan giggled. "I doubt it, Jacob." She turned to Daniel. "What say you?"

"None of them, I'm sorry to report. This outbuilding is Alster Tower, and because it has two bowling lanes, a billiard room, and more, it's nicknamed the Playhouse." He drove the skiff around the shoreline and motioned toward another small stone structure in the water. "This is the Powerhouse and Clock Tower."

He shut off the engine and directed their attention toward the main building. "In Boldt Castle, there are a hundred and twenty rooms, thirty-one fireplaces, and thirty bathrooms. I bet it'd be fun to play hide-and-seek in there, aye?"

Jacob and Joseph agreed, but Jacob indicated the building behind him. "I'd rather go bowling. Never have."

Reagan dipped her head. "Well, perhaps you will one day."

Before Daniel started up the engine again, he added some important history to the tour. "Mr. Boldt was a German immigrant and was so partial to the castles in his homeland that he built this castle for his wife. He even reshaped the island to look like a heart—because he loved her so much." Without thinking, he snapped an adoring glance at Reagan, who promptly turned a pretty pink.

The boys started making kissing noises and pretended to hug the air.

"Settle down, lads." Daniel grimaced to make his next point clear. "But, tragically, Louisa Boldt died before it was finished, so they never lived there."

Reagan's eyes misted. "That's so sad."

"Yes, but it still stands as a testimony of his love for her. I think that commendable." Daniel kept his eyes on the river ahead and started the engine. If he looked at Reagan, his words might betray his growing feelings for her.

"Hold on, and I'll take you for a fast ride." Just as his heart raced, he eased into the main shipping channel and opened the engine wide, heading back toward Cherry Island. The twins squealed with delight, and Reagan's smile affirmed she enjoyed it too. But soon, he slowed the skiff to normal speed.

"We're edging Frontenac Shoal and must be wary of how we traverse this river. The shipping channel is deep, but shallow, rocky shoals have caused a great many ships, large and small, to go down." A large freighter headed downriver, blocking their view of the bay. But when it passed, they were parallel to Casino Island.

Joseph pointed. "Isn't that where we saw the fireworks?"

Daniel grinned. "How did you get to be so smart? There are bowling alleys in the facilities there, too, but you have to be a guest of the Thousand Island House to use them." He winked at Jacob, who pulled his shoulders back as he answered with bravado.

"When I grow up, I'm gonna stay at the hotel and go bowling."

Now to have some fun with the boys. "I think we have time to see the Devil's Oven. How does that sound?" Daniel added as much mystery as he could muster in his deep voice.

Reagan's brow furrowed, so Daniel gave her a wink. Hopefully, she'd play along.

"Sounds spooky. Are we safe going there?" Joining his plan, she nudged Joseph with her elbow.

"Sure! We're not scared." The boys grinned, sitting up straight and brave as they passed between the mainland and Cherry Island, but then Jacob's enthusiasm faltered. "Hey, you said we were going to that Devil's Island place. Not home."

Daniel pretended to pull up to the dock at the boathouse but then eased away and saluted the island. "See you soon, Casa Blanca. We have one more stop to make."

Jacob waved a hand at him. "Awww, Mr. Daniel. You were trickin' us."

Daniel chuckled, and Reagan joined in with her tinkling-bell giggle. "I love your laugh, Miss Reagan. Reminds me of my mother's."

There it was again. That blush he enjoyed seeing.

"We're coming up on Devil's Oven, lads. Now be on the lookout. There are stories of pirates and bandits who hide in the cave. Way back during the 1830s Patriot War, a pirate named Bill Johnson is said to have hidden there for months after he looted a British steamer, *Sir Robert Peel*. Let's see if we can catch sight of any modern-day pirates. Quiet, now."

Dramatically, Daniel turned the boat toward the cave and shut off the engine. The boys were whisper quiet, but when the boat drifted within feet of the cave opening, Joseph stood up and shouted, "Get us out of here! They might come after us and capture us!"

"I was just having a bit of fun with you, laddie. There are no pirates in there."

Joseph blew out a relieved breath and plunked down in his seat. "Oh."

When they returned to Cherry Island, Daniel handed the boys poles to fish off the dock. He offered Reagan an Adirondack loveseat, and she scooted into it, tucking her skirts beside her. He joined her. "That'll occupy them for a few moments."

"Thank you for the tour. It was magnificent." Reagan patted the back of his hand, but he quickly turned it over and took her tiny hand in his.

"I enjoyed hearing how the lads answered your questions. I'd forgotten how special the Shabbat symbolism is. Father never bothered with it." Daniel's voice cracked.

"I can't help but see Jesus in all of it. He said He was the Light of the World and the Bread of Life. He took the cup of wine and said, 'this is My blood of the covenant.' His body was even wrapped with spices like in the little box the boys talked about. Can you not see how Jesus fulfills all this?"

Daniel gazed at the sparkling river. "We Jews have been waiting for the Messiah for so long."

"But He's already come. Jesus came and fulfilled it all." Reagan touched his forearm, giving it a soft pat before returning her hand to her lap.

"I caught one, Mr. Daniel!" Jacob's pole bowed, so Daniel ran to help.

"Aye. You've got a bullhead, Jacob." He removed the fish and threw it into the river.

"Hey, what did you do that for?"

"It's too small, and sometimes it's best just to fish for fun." He returned Jacob's pole to him and hurried back to Reagan. "I think I understand. Perhaps my mother's faith, your faith, is the true faith."

Reagan reached for his hand and squeezed it. "It's not because it's hers or mine. It's that the Messiah came and brought us all hope for our future. And that faith can be yours too."

Daniel's eyes misted as her words sunk deep in his mind and heart.

## Chapter 11

A week later, Reagan led the boys into an empty dining room. Where were the Bernheims?

"Guess we're early for breakfast." Joseph plunked down in his seat, laying his head on the table.

"Your uncle and aunt should be here any minute. Patience is a virtue. Remember?" Reagan ruffled Joseph's hair.

"What are these?" Jacob slipped on his uncle's spectacles. His brow furrowed as he stared at his plate. "I didn't know that was a *B*. I thought it was just a squiggly design."

Now Reagan's brow furrowed. Could it be? She scooted out of her chair and scurried to the living room to get the newspaper she'd seen on the table. She returned and handed it to Jacob. "Read this."

Jacob took the paper. "*Watertown Daily Times.*" He grinned wide. "Hey, look at this. I can see the words plain as day. 'America wins the Olympiad. Vic-tor-ious Athletes Receive Prizes from King. James Thorpe, the Carl-isle Indian, carries Old Glory to Victory in the De-cath-alon.' What's that, Miss Reagan?"

Reagan closed her dropped jaw before she answered him. "Jacob. You can read! You just needed glasses."

Jacob stared at her until his eyes brimmed with tears. "I'm not stupid?"

Reagan shook her head violently and hugged the boy. "*No!* You are *not* stupid. Look at those multi-syllable words you read."

Just then, Mr. and Mrs. Bernheim entered the room and took their seats. When Mr. Bernheim saw Jacob with his glasses, he snatched them from his face. "Those are not toys, son."

"But I can see, Uncle. I can read!" Jacob swiped at the tears that had slipped onto his cheeks.

Mr. Bernheim turned to Reagan. "What's the meaning of this?"

"It is true, sir. Jacob has struggled with reading, but when he put on your spectacles, he could read just fine." Her voice was so high-pitched, she barely recognized it.

"Well, now. I had that very thing happen to me when I was your age." Mr. Bernheim smirked and left the room. The boys took a sip of their juice, the women their coffee, and none said a word about the man's departure. Was he coming back?

When he returned, Mr. Bernheim waved a smaller pair of glasses in the air. "I didn't know why I kept these until now. They were mine when I was a boy. You may have them." He handed Jacob a tiny pair of wire-rimmed spectacles, and the child put them on. They fit perfectly.

Jacob jumped up from his chair and hugged his uncle. "Thank you ever so much, Uncle!" He sat back down, picked up the paper, and pointed to a photograph of a man running. "Did you know this man won an Olympic medal?" He trailed his finger over the text beneath the picture, his lips moving. "I can see all the letters just fine! Thank you, sir."

Mr. Bernheim snapped his napkin open and placed it in his lap. "You're very welcome."

"That's great, Jake. I'm happy for you." Joseph's continued kindness warmed Reagan's heart.

By now, all five of them were teary-eyed but smiling. Mr. Bernheim cleared his throat and shifted in his seat. After several moments, he bowed his head, prayed a blessing, and started to eat in silence.

Mrs. Bernheim opened the conversation by asking the boys what they had been learning lately.

Joseph waved his fork in the air. "Miss Reagan has taught us all kinds of things. Astronomy … that's when you see the constellations and such. Horticulture … that's about growing plants and taking care of gardens like Mr. Daniel does. And photosynthesis … that's how plants take in light and water and stuff so they can grow." He beamed before taking a bite of his eggs.

As his brother chewed, Jacob joined in. "And she taught us how to draw things, like you are teaching us the piano, Auntie. We even got to learn about ships and sloops and windjammers, and about zoology. I'm going to be a zookeeper and take care of animals when I grow up."

Mr. Bernheim chuckled. "Are you, now?" He cleared his throat before turning to his wife. "It appears you made the right choice for the twins' tutelage after all, Mrs. Bernheim. Well done!" Then he addressed Reagan. "And you, too, miss."

Reagan's cheeks warmed at his rare moment of praise. "Thank you, sir. They've been a delight to care for."

Mrs. Bernheim tittered. "Well, most of the time." She tossed Reagan a knowing grin, and Reagan affirmed their secrets with a slight nod.

"I'm off to the city, but I'll be back in a week for your birthday, boys." Mr. Bernheim's casual demeanor surprised Reagan. He'd been so aloof for so long that she wasn't sure how to take it.

Mrs. Bernheim smiled. "We shall fare fine, *mein liba*. Miss Reagan has things well in hand, and both boys can now enjoy our vast library." She glanced at Jacob and winked.

"Can we read *Robinson Crusoe*, Miss Reagan? I've always wanted to."

Reagan set her teacup down. "Of course, Jacob. We'll start on it this very day."

Mr. Bernheim turned the conversation. "But how will you fare without a maid, wife?"

What? Etta was gone? How did she miss that?

The missus waved a hand. "Mrs. Rosenstein has already agreed to lend a hand until you bring me a new maid from the city. We live simply here, and I don't need much fussing."

"If you're sure. I'll find a new maid for you this week."

"Yes, I'm sure. Thank you, husband." Mrs. Bernheim poured another cup of coffee.

Joseph quirked a brow. "Miss Etta is gone? She was pretty, but she wasn't very nice."

Reagan patted his hand and leaned in to whisper in his ear. "Let's be charitable, and this is none of your concern."

When breakfast concluded, Reagan took the boys up to her room for some classroom time. They read from their *McGuffy Reader*s, did some math problems, and tried to work on perfect Palmer penmanship.

"I like cursive, Miss Reagan. It's like drawing." Joseph bit his tongue as he worked on forming his words with uniform, rhythmic grace.

"Everything's easier with my new spectacles, Miss Reagan. I didn't know it could be so simple." Jacob squinched up his nose, freckles and all, as he worked on his writing. "Look how good I'm doing!"

Reagan surveyed his work, and yes! It was as if she had an entirely new boy in her class. Why hadn't she realized he needed glasses? Why hadn't his instructors at that fancy New York City school of his? With much praise and a prayer on her lips, she thanked God that Jacob had put on his uncle's spectacles when he did.

"Beautiful, Jacob." Reagan paused and tapped her cheek. "Let's stop here. I think we should go and try our hand at drawing the stained-glass pheasants in the hallway. Been meaning to do that for weeks."

The twins closed their composition books and stood, paper and pencil in hand. "That sounds like fun,

Miss Reagan." Jacob wiggled in front of Joseph, probably wanting the prime seat.

Reagan rolled her eyes and picked up her sketch pad, pencil, and crayons. "The window is so colorful that we'll use the crayons so we can color our drawings."

She opened the door, and just a dozen feet away was their subject—a stunning, stained-glass window just on the other side of the staircase. It sported a picture of two colorful pheasants among wispy, flowering branches, ornately framed with colorful glass designs. When the sun shone through it, the colors came alive, a glorious sight.

Reagan motioned to the wooden floor before them. "Let's sit here and begin with the frame. Try and use the whole page to capture the intricate patterns of the outside first, then we'll work on the pheasants and the flowers." Reagan taught them a little about perspective, dimension, and scale. For nearly an hour, both boys sat quiet and still, concentrating on making their drawings into masterpieces.

"This is fun, Miss Reagan." Joseph finished the frame and busily colored in his pheasants, trying to shade the blues and greens to create the teal on the birds' wings. "But the colors don't work. They're not the same."

Reagan squatted to view his work. "It's lovely, Joseph. Art isn't about duplicating the subject perfectly. It's about making it yours."

Jacob held his paper up. "Look at mine, teacher!"

How she loved being called *teacher*! There was something magical about the name.

"It's wonderful, and so artistic." Though his scale of the birds wasn't quite right, Reagan praised him for his use of color and perspective.

When they were done, it was time to read. "Let's go out to the gazebo and get some fresh air. Then we can start reading *Robinson Crusoe*."

Quick as a wink, the boys closed their composition books, ran to the room to drop off their supplies, and stood in the hallway waiting for her.

"My, but you two are quick! Jacob, would you run these to my desk, please?" She handed the boy her supplies, and he flew to complete the task.

Reagan led them downstairs and slipped the novel from its spot on the bookshelves. Outside, a warm breeze kissed her cheeks.

"Take the book and leave it at the gazebo. You may run and play for ten minutes, and I'll meet you there presently." Smiling, she shooed the boys away.

Like happy little jackrabbits, the twins ran and jumped and chased each other, taking a rather circuitous route to the gazebo. When she got there, they were already sitting on the chaise together, Jacob reading the tale of *Robinson Crusoe*.

Reagan stood just outside the gazebo, marveling how one simple pair of spectacles could change a person so quickly and give him confidence to do what he'd feared doing just the day before. Her heart brimmed with joy.

"Top of the morning, lass. And how are we faring this fine day?" Daniel slipped beside her, quiet as a mouse, like he often did. She didn't even flinch this time.

"Faring better than fine!" Reagan filled him in on the morning's miracles, giggling with happiness at the events of the past few hours.

~ ~ ~

Daniel's heart abounded with love for the woman before him as she shared her story. With Etta gone, and now this, it was a fine day, indeed.

"Aye, that's crackers, lass. And to think a bit of glass could turn a scrappy lad into a bookworm." Daniel rubbed his chin as he entered the gazebo. "Why, Sir Jacob, you look like a grand Jewish scholar. Wherever did you find such dandy spectacles?"

"They were Uncle's, and they help me read." Jacob grinned but went right back to reading without another word. Daniel returned to Reagan, who now sat under a large maple tree, positioned so she could watch the boys.

Daniel took a seat on the ground beside her. He scanned the river and pointed as a windjammer passed by the island, birds chirping in the trees above them. "She's a beauty. I'd love to sail on one of those someday."

Reagan tilted her head. "She is lovely. And what's new with you?"

Daniel kept his eyes on the boat as he answered her. "I've been pondering our conversations of late, about faith. Remembering the security Mama found in hers and thinking about what I see in you."

Reagan reached over and touched his forearm, awaking his nerves. "I don't have it all figured out, but I know God is the Creator, the Savior, and the One who loves me."

Daniel slipped a tiny Bible out of his pocket and waved it in the air. "I bought this at Cornwall Brothers just last week. I've been reading the Psalms and found them especially enlightening, so I've been praying a certain passage for days now. 'Teach me thy way, O Lord; I will walk in thy truth; unite my heart to fear thy name.'" He turned to her, searching her face for what she thought. "I want to know truth."

Reagan slipped her arm into his and gave it a squeeze. "Then you will find it. If you search for Him, you will."

"Miss Reagan, what's this word?" Joseph pointed to his book, so Reagan tried to stand to go and help him. Somehow, she caught her heel on her skirts and lost her balance, falling into Daniel's arms, her long, dark lashes tickling his cheek and her lemon verbena scent swirling to his nose.

An inch. Just an inch between their lips. Oh, how he wanted to taste them! But he quickly realized that the boys were watching and that she was paralyzed in such an awkward position. He took hold of her shoulders and set her aright, securely on the ground. He then scooted onto his knees, stood, and lifted her up as if she were a small child. Light as a feather, she was, yet perhaps it was the adrenaline racing through his body that gave him such strength.

Once they were both firmly on their feet, Reagan brushed the grass and leaves from her dress and hurried to the boys, who covered their snickering mouths with their hands, their eyes dancing with merriment. She quickly answered Jacob's question and then bid them to run and play tag before they could comment on her mishap.

The boys complied, darting up the hill and tagging each other every two seconds.

"Goodness! I'm sorry for losing my balance. That was quite a scene. I'm just glad Etta wasn't around." Reagan swiped at the perspiration forming on her brow, her cheeks rosy and her eyes flustered.

Daniel turned to her and took her hand. "There, there, my *stoirín*. When I shuttled Etta to the bay, she had steam spewing from each ear, so mad she was!" He paused to admire Reagan's dancing eyes. "We needn't be on tenterhooks any longer since we haven't her prying eyes to worry about."

Reagan sighed. "But we do have two small pairs of eyes and plenty of others on the island. We must take care to not create controversy." She paused, quirking a brow. "What's *stoirin*?"

"It's Irish and it means, 'my precious treasure.' Mama always called me that." He kissed her hands before letting them go. "I agree we must take care not to cause scandal." He glanced at the boys and gulped. "But I think I must tussle with the twins to settle my insides." He had to expend the nervous energy from having her so close, so intimately close.

Reagan giggled as Daniel sprinted to the boys, grabbed the two of them, and gently tossed them to the ground, wrestling with both of them simultaneously as he ignored her gaze on them. They pulled at his limbs and tried their best to overcome him, but they were no match. For several minutes, the three laughed and scuffled, enjoying pure fun as boys often do, until all three of them were winded and weary.

"Are you rascals quite finished?" Reagan stood over them, hands on her hips, an amused grin on her face. "It's nearly time for lunch, and you two have some cleaning up to do before your aunt sees you. Now, skedaddle!"

Jacob and Joseph guffawed, thanked Daniel for the fun, and raced to the house. Reagan called after them. "Quiet in the house, boys. Be gentlemen."

Daniel wiped the sweat from his brow. "Seems you have the two leprechauns wrapped around your pretty little finger."

"I hope so. But I better go and make sure." Reagan's eyes flashed with mirth as she turned toward Casa Blanca.

~ ~ ~

As Reagan had watched Daniel with the twins, dreams of him playing with *their* children had warmed her heart, set her mind spinning. She could no longer deny her feelings for him. Was it love?

But no! Though Daniel was open now, he was still just searching, and without a shared faith, a future with him was unthinkable. They were too different. In the past few months, her faith had become the underpinning of her life, the very foundation on which she stood. She just couldn't allow anything, even love, to shake that foundation.

With a deep sigh, she entered the house, navigated the staircase, knocked on the boys' door, and entered their room, where she found them already changed into clean clothes and combing their hair. "My perfect gentlemen. Well done! You look ready to meet the Queen."

"What queen, Miss Reagan?" At Joseph's innocent question, she held back her amusement. The boy too often took things literally.

Reagan adjusted his crooked suspenders. "Oh, that's just an expression. But your aunt will be pleased to see you so."

Mrs. Bernheim was already seated when they entered the dining room. She acknowledged them as they sat. "You boys look mighty nice. But where are your spectacles, Jacob?"

Jacob's face turned white as the tablecloth. "Oh, dear! I left them in the grass!" Without asking, he scurried out the door.

Mrs. Bernheim prayed, and they began to eat without waiting for him. Suddenly, they heard, "Help! Fire!" Was that Jacob?

The three of them jumped from their seats and hurried onto the veranda. Sure enough, a small grass fire burned on a knoll near the gazebo. Daniel, already on site, slapped the fire with a wet blanket.

Jacob ran to them and hugged Reagan. "I'm sorry. I took my spectacles off so they wouldn't get broken while we played. I don't know how the fire started. Honest, Miss Reagan. But they're not hurt. See?" He showed her the undamaged spectacles.

Reagan kissed the top of the boy's head, feeling him tremble underneath her. "There, there. How could you know that your spectacles could focus the light and bend it to make a fire in the dry grass and leaves lying around? That's called combustion."

They watched as Daniel put out the small fire and came their way. "All better. That was a wee bit scary, aye, Jacob?"

258

Jacob sniffed back his tears and wiped his eyes with his fist. Letting go of Reagan, he stepped back and sucked in a settling breath. "That was combustion."

Daniel snorted and slapped his thigh. "Does everything have to be a lesson, Miss Reagan?"

"But of course. All of life is a series of lessons that we can learn and grow from." She turned to Jacob. "What did you learn today, sweet boy?"

"Never, ever, ever leave my spectacles in the sun."

Reagan ruffled his hair. "Lesson learned." Maybe she had a few lessons to learn as well. About keeping a better eye on the boy's spectacles. About being careful with her heart. And maybe, about love.

## Chapter 12

Reagan couldn't stop grinning. Her secret just itched to be set free, but she'd have to hold it in a few more minutes. "Come on, birthday boys. Your aunt is waiting for you."

"I'm hurrying, Miss Reagan." Jacob struggled to comb his thick hair.

"May I?" Reagan took the comb and smoothed his stubborn cowlick back into place. "All better. But look at those dirty spectacles!" She swished them under the water faucet, dried them, and handed them back to Jacob. Then she bent down and whispered, "By the way, I just love your freckles, young man."

Jacob beamed, a slight blush coloring his cheeks.

"I'm hungry." Joseph whined as he stood at the door.

When Reagan and Jacob joined him, Reagan took a moment to give him a hug. "Thanks for waiting, Joseph. You're such a fine young gentleman."

Joseph licked his lips as he led the way. "I hope we'll have flapjacks for our birthday breakfast."

"Me too. Feel any older JoeJoe? I do!" Jacob glanced back at his brother before taking the last two steps in one smooth bound, nearly bumping into his aunt.

"Careful, now." Mrs. Bernheim grinned. "Happy birthday, boys."

Once they had sat down at the dining room table, prayed a blessing, and begun to eat their flapjacks, Mrs. Bernheim set down her fork. "I have an announcement." She winked at Reagan. "We have a special surprise for you today. Your uncle and I have arranged a birthday celebration on Casino Island, including bowling—since I hear you'd like that." She smiled at the boys, who looked like two overblown balloons ready to burst. "Your uncle will meet us there at two o'clock sharp, and we shall have an afternoon of it, packed with birthday cake and games."

The boys jumped up from their chairs and ran to hug their aunt. Reagan giggled at the scene. How things had changed through the summer—for all of them! Just now, she wished she had one of those fancy cameras to capture the moment.

"I love you, Auntie! You're the best!" Joseph kissed his aunt on her cheek, and Jacob followed.

As the boys returned to their seats, their aunt rubbed her temples and frowned. Hopefully, the mistress isn't nursing one of her headaches again on the boys' special day.

Reagan indicated for each of the boys to put their napkins on their laps. "How many nine-year-olds get such a special birthday? August 11, 1912, will be a day you'll remember forever."

"I've wanted to bowl my whole life." Jacob poked a piece of flapjack with his fork and held it in midair. "This will be the best birthday ever." He stuck the morsel in his mouth and chewed happily.

For the next few minutes, the boys told about their other birthdays in New York City. Reagan marveled at their special memories of touring the Statue of Liberty, watching *A Trip to Chinatown* on Broadway, even traveling to Washington, D.C., last year. She could only imagine experiencing such wonders, so how could bowling truly be the best birthday ever?

When breakfast was over, Mrs. Bernheim invited them to join her on the veranda where a single, wrapped package and a pure white envelope lay on the wicker table. "A gift from your mother and father."

The twins' eyes twinkled with delight. They sat on the wicker loveseat like little gentlemen as they waited for Reagan and Mrs. Bernheim to join them. Reagan wondered at their fortitude in not tearing into the package.

"I'll read the card, and you can open the package, okay, JoeJoe?" Jacob ceremoniously opened the envelope and removed an intricately drawn card with two puppies jumping up to pop balloons, the words, "Happy Birthday" dramatically embellished above the artwork. Reagan had never seen such a beautiful card.

Jacob adjusted his spectacles and read aloud.

"'Dearest Jacob and Joseph, Happy ninth birthday, my darling boys. How we wish we could celebrate your special day with you. But your aunt and uncle have arranged an outing, and we hope this gift will bring you much pleasure. We will return from our voyage in two weeks and will be overjoyed by our reunion with you, our precious sons. All our love and devotion, Mother and Daddy.'"

*My service as governess will be over in two short weeks, and then what?* Reagan's heart hit the floor at the thought of the looming changes ahead.

Joseph took the card and hugged it before setting it on the table. "Let's see what's in here." The child slowly slipped off the string and removed the brown paper to reveal a board game. *"Pirate and Traveler.* This looks like fun. Wanna play, Auntie?"

Mrs. Bernheim shook her head. "I'm sorry, boys, but I have a headache and should lie down before we go to your party. Please excuse me." She stood and kissed each boy on the top of his head then promptly disappeared into the house.

"Wanna play with us, Mr. Daniel?" Jacob hollered at Daniel, who was walking toward Casa Blanca, hedge clippers in hand. He gave a wave and joined them on the veranda.

"We got a new game for our birthday!" Joseph picked it up and shook the box.

"Happy birthday, boys." Daniel sat where Mrs. Bernheim had. He nodded Reagan's way and gifted her with a handsome smile. "Miss Reagan."

Daniel reached for the game and showed it to Reagan. On the cover, colorful artwork of a smiling pirate, a ship on an angry ocean, and a treasure chest was accompanied by the words, *Pirate and Traveler, Amusement and Instruction for the Greatest of all Games.*

Daniel chuckled. "How can I say no to the greatest of all games?" He handed the box to Joseph, who opened it to find a map of the world, travel cards, a spinner, pawns, and instructions. Once they read the rules, they played the game … twice. Soon it was nearly time for the noon meal.

"Well, laddies, you've distracted me a wee bit too much. I'd best be about my work before I take you to your party. See you soon." Daniel stood and waved before scooping up his clippers and chopping away at the overgrown hedge along the path.

~ ~ ~

Later that day, Reagan followed Daniel and two excited boys up the hill toward the Thousand Island House recreational facility on Casino Island. The three-story building appeared much more striking in the sunshine, and while she'd never even seen a bowling alley, watching the twins' faces when they did would bring her much pleasure.

She hurried to catch up with the two, not wanting to miss a moment of their exuberance. Upon entering the building, signs for game room, billiard room, bowling alley, children's nursery, men's and women's bathing room, swimming pool, and dancing pavilion made her head swim. How could one choose from such entertainment?

Mr. Bernheim stood at the front desk and motioned for them to join him. "Welcome, and happy birthday, nephews! I hope this will be a memorable day."

Joseph and Jacob ran up to him and embraced him generously. Jacob said, "Thank you for this, Uncle!" and Joseph added to his brother's salutation.

Their uncle had to peel them off of him. "Where's Mrs. Bernheim?"

Reagan curtsied. "I'm sorry to say that a headache plagued her, and she had to decline joining us. She asked to beg your forgiveness."

Mr. Bernheim shook his head, frowning. "They besiege her far too often these days. I should check on her momentarily." He rubbed his chin, apparently pondering something. "I'll tell you what. Let's adjust our schedule of festivities. I will stay for bowling and cake. Then, Daniel, you can return me to the island while the boys swim and play to their hearts' content."

"Very good, sir." Daniel gave him a slight bow. How elegant Daniel could be, and then in the wink of an eye, he could become a simple boatman or wrestle with little boys. She could imagine herself living her life with such a man, curling up with him and talking by the fire on a winter's evening, raising children with him, growing old with him.

"This way to the bowling alleys." Mr. Bernheim swept a hand toward the facilities, and an hour of noisy, high-spirited amusement began. Mr. Bernheim shed his coat and showed the boys the rules and techniques of bowling while she and Daniel laughed and cheered them on. Never had she seen the man so casually engaged with the twins, and she took great joy in observing it.

Jacob caught on quickly, taking the appropriate steps and releasing the ball at just the right moment. But poor Joseph struggled, even dropping the heavy ball twice before he even got to the line to release it. His uncle forbade tears but encouraged him, yet the child's frown lingered.

Once, Joseph came and sat close to Reagan, leaning against her for comfort. She smoothed his hair.

"Fear not, sweet boy. We all have our strengths and weaknesses. It's okay if you don't enjoy the game."

He turned his head and rubbed his face on her sleeve. "I hate it."

"Come, Joseph. It's your last try." Mr. Bernheim beckoned him from the lane.

Joseph rolled his eyes and stepped up to the mark. He sucked in a breath and gave it his best, releasing the ball just right. It rolled right down the middle and slammed every pin down!

"Strike! I got a strike!" Joseph danced and whooped and hollered until his uncle had to grab him into a hug to settle him down.

Jacob slapped him on the back. "I knew you could do it, JoeJoe!"

Gloom turned to joy, and it was time for cake. Mr. Bernheim led them to the dining room and even invited

Daniel to join them. When they were all seated, a waiter served them a layered orange sponge cake with pecans on top and tart lemonade with raspberries floating in it. How elegant!

Best of all, the twins seemed to be relishing the time with their uncle, chatting gaily about bowling and dreams of the future. They told him about the game of *Pirate and Traveler* and thanked him profusely for this special day.

When they'd finished their cake, Mr. Bernheim stood to leave. "I'm sorry to say, boys, that I need to return to the island and see to your aunt. You may enjoy the facilities as long as you'd like; just be back before dark. And you must behave for Miss Reagan, or she shall bring you home early, and I shall deal with you accordingly. Is that understood, nephews?"

Jacob and Joseph bobbed their heads, and in unison said, "Yes, sir!"

Reagan covered a giggle with her napkin. Those two could be so different and so alike all within a hummingbird's flutter.

~ ~ ~

That evening after Reagan tucked the twins into bed—exhausted from an afternoon of water games in the pool—Daniel stood beside her on the veranda as the sun retreated slowly, casting a heavenly rainbow of yellow, orange, and peach over the river. His heart thudded as he faced her. "What a magical day for those boys. And now, for a magical evening. Shall we walk? I have things to say."

Reagan slipped her hand into the crook of his offered arm. "I just love watching the sun set over this river, don't you? It's so enchanting that it makes me want to cry."

"I've come to appreciate all things beautiful of late. But please don't cry. I'd rather face a den of lions than a woman's tears." He winked at her, hoping she knew his comment was in jest.

"We couldn't have that, now, could we?" Reagan's expression of joy, her sparkling eyes captivated him. "What did you want to say tonight, kind sir?"

Daniel led her to the lion's arch and down the steps to the grassy moat. Then he cleared his throat and took both of her hands in his. "I have asked Jesus to be my savior, and I feel a peace beyond anything I could ever have imagined." He pulled out his small Bible and continued. "I've been reading this every spare moment and find it fascinating. Last night, I read the book of Ruth." He opened the Bible, flipped through its pages, and read to her. "'Entreat me not to leave thee, or to return from following after thee: for whither though goest, I will go; and where thou lodgest, I will lodge; thy people shall be my people, and thy God my God.'"

Reagan's brows furrowed, and she tilted her head. "That's … nice. But I must admit that I haven't read that particular book."

Daniel blew out a breath. "What I mean to say is that I love you, Reagan, and I want your God to be my God, and I never want to leave your side and—and … will you marry me?" He plopped down on one knee and implored her with all the emotion inside of him, kissing her tiny hands. He withdrew his mother's ring from his pocket and presented it to her. "This is for our wedding day!"

As the setting sun bathed her in the warmest pink glow he'd ever seen, Reagan's eyes brimmed with tears, and for several eternal seconds, he thought she was going to decline. But then, her face mirrored the glowing violet and then crimson, and her wide, warm smile lit up his heart. Her eyes danced a waltz, and the flecks of gold seemed to glow within silvery pools of joy. "Yes! Oh, a thousand times, yes!"

Daniel stood, slipped the ring back into his pocket, and gently took her face in his hands. Her skin was soft to his touch, and she smelled of lemon verbena and hope for the future. "Good, because I have taken the liberty of wiring your parents to receive their permission to marry you. I have also taken the permanent, full-time apprenticeship with Solicitor Goodwin. And last, but not least, I have secured you an interview for the position of teacher at Alexandria Bay Grammar School."

"You did all that? For me? Oh, Daniel! What a gift and a reward from the Almighty you are! I love you." She leaned in and kissed him passionately. He deepened her kiss, caressing her face, her hair, hugging her tightly as if this angel might fly away. He breathed her breath, felt her heart beating in her chest almost to the same rhythm as his. But then he tenderly pulled away—else he might not survive another minute.

"That ... that was more magical than any sunset or the sweetest rose or the freshest fish dinner." His words came out in a whoosh.

"My kiss was better than fish? Really, my love." Reagan stepped back and placed her hands on her hips in mock offense.

Daniel rolled his eyes. "Beg pardon. Let's try that again." He scooped her into a tight embrace and rewarded her with the deepest, most passionate kiss he could muster. When he finished, he dropped his arms and stepped back, grinning like a fool. She licked her lips and stared at him as if stunned. Silence ensued, and Daniel's heartbeat stuttered. Had he been too forward? Offended her?

"Heavenly. Truly." Reagan barely breathed the words. Then she blinked as if coming out of a trance. Her brows furrowed, fear flashing in her eyes. "What ... what will the Bernheims think? I don't want any scandal to mar my letter of recommendation."

Daniel grinned. "Oh, that. I've already spoken to the missus about my intentions and given my notice to leave their employ. She was overjoyed about our impending nuptials."

Reagan pursed her lips and shook her head. "How long have you been gambling, planning, and plotting this, dearest?"

"Almost since the day I met you, love."

~ ~ ~

Reagan returned to the house with a bright, new future in her forecast. Her face ached from grinning, but she felt like a hummingbird—weightless, soaring, beautiful—her heart beating so fast she feared she'd wake the Bernheims with its thumping. But she jumped and gasped when she walked by the living room and found Mrs. Bernheim sitting on the sofa.

"I thought you'd never come inside. Where were you, miss?" The missus pasted on a stern demeanor, but her sparkling eyes betrayed her ruse.

Reagan shrugged. "Mr. Lovitz and I were talking, 'tis all."

Mrs. Bernheim clicked her tongue, rolling her eyes. "And what, pray tell, were you discussing in the dark?"

"I … he … he asked me to marry him." Reagan lowered her eyes at her confession.

"I knew it! Congratulations!" Mrs. Bernheim stood and held out a black velvet box. "An engagement gift for you."

Reagan blinked, tilting her head. She blew out a steadying breath and took the box, slowly and reverently opened it. At seeing its contents, she bit her bottom lip to hold back the tears. "Oh, Mrs. Bernheim, it's exquisite!"

The brooch was an intricately carved, white alabaster cameo of a woman's profile set in pink and framed in costly gold filigree. A rare gift. "This is too extravagant a gift for me, missus."

Mrs. Bernheim groaned. "Stuff and nonsense. Alabaster symbolizes purity and is said to protect an innocent heart. I found this brooch on one of my trips to Cuba, and though I treasure it, I want you to have it always and to wear on your wedding day and remember your time at Casa Blanca with us and the twins. And Mr. Lovitz, of course."

Reagan giggled. "Thank you ever so much." She closed the box and cradled it against her heart. "I will, missus. I shall treasure it forever—the memories, the love—all of it!"

## Epilogue

**December 24, 1912**

Reagan welcomed Daniel into the lobby of the Crossmon Hotel, where she'd been lodging for the past four months as she taught. He shook the snow from his hat and brushed fat flakes from his overcoat before unbuttoning and removing it. He gave it another good shake.

Reagan giggled as she led him to a nearby loveseat and bid him to sit. She kissed his cheek. "Nothing could dampen this day, not even this snowstorm. The children are home for the holidays, and I'm ready to wed, dearest Daniel. Thank you for waiting so I could have this one season of teaching under me."

"And your last day in the lap of luxury, miss." Daniel glanced around the elegant hotel lavishly decorated for Christmas. "Soon, you'll be all mine!"

Reagan's eye twinkled. "It was gracious for the school board to house me here, but I can't wait to make my home with you." She took his hand and squeezed it.

Daniel squeezed back and then held her hands to his lips and kissed them slowly, lingering over them, a habit she'd come to relish. "Mr. Goodwin's cottage may not be fancy, but it will be ours. I think I've made the house ready, but your loving, womanly touches will make it our home. I hope you'll be pleased."

Reagan tilted her head. "You've kept me in the dark for far too long, sir. I'm itching to *finally* see it."

"I had to have a project to busy my hands these four eternal months, miss!" Daniel chuckled. "But it shall be the Lovitz love nest in short order."

The wind howled fiercely outside the window behind them, and they both turned to look, bumping heads in the process. They laughed at the mishap. Beyond the pane, the white flakes fell steady and strong, evoking a frown from Daniel. "It's getting worse. I fear your family mightn't make it to the wedding with all this snow. Should we postpone the service?"

"No! Not another day! All I want for Christmas is you, dearest Daniel Lovitz, and if they can't make it, I'll be happy if our wedding is no more than Pastor Mark and us. We can always celebrate with them another time." Reagan held back the tears that stung the back of her eyes. Their nuptials simply must happen this very night!

"Telegrams, miss." The front desk attendant delivered to her not one, but two missives. She gave one that was addressed to the both of them to Daniel and slowly opened hers.

She read aloud. "'Trains snowbound. Stop. Will miss your wedding. Stop. Carry on. Stop. Mama and Father.'" Reagan's eyes misted over. "Well, that's that. I have prepared for this eventuality ever since it began to snow so hard."

Daniel reached for her hand and kissed it. "Still, I am sorry, my love." He opened the second telegram and scanned it, raising his eyebrows. "It's from the Bernheims. 'Wedding gift. Stop. New York City honeymoon. Stop. Tickets and instructions at station. Stop. All expenses paid. Stop. The Bernheims.'"

Reagan bit her lip as she comprehended the gift. She gazed at an equally stunned Daniel. "Can this be real,

Daniel? The Bernheims would do this for us, their lowly servants?"

Daniel shrugged. "I'm as perplexed as you, my bride-to-be. But that's what it says. I'd better go to the station and gather the information. And you, my dear girl, must pack for your honeymoon."

Reagan stood and planted her hands on her hips. "You're the one who must pack, my husband-to-be. I already did, remember?"

Daniel guffawed. "That's right. Seems you, my dear, are way ahead of me." He bent down and kissed her on the lips, several guests gasping with disapproval. He turned to them and threw his hands in the air. "Sorry, I'm marrying this woman tonight!" He let out a whoop, and the guests laughed at his antics.

Reagan just shook her head.

Daniel slipped on his still-wet overcoat and plopped his hat on his head. "See you at the altar, my bride! I love you."

"And I love you." Reagan pecked him on the cheek and waved him out into the snowstorm. *Will anyone come to our wedding on such a blustery eve?* She didn't know, nor, truthfully, did she care.

~ ~ ~

Daniel tugged on the tails that Mr. Goodwin had lent him. He marveled at the fit and grinned as he smoothed down his hair. A knock on the door startled him.

Opening it, he found Solicitor Goodwin standing there, stomping snow from his feet. "May I come in, please?"

Daniel opened the door wide. "Of course, sir. Would you like some tea?"

Mr. Goodwin shook his head, his brown eyes dancing in the candlelight. "It's quite a storm, eh, my fine young man?"

"That it is. Very blustery." Daniel waited for the rest of the man's speech, for by now, he could tell when the man had more to say.

"I hope you don't mind, but Pastor Mark came to me earlier today, worried about your nuptials. We agreed to move the festivities from our humble church to the Crossmon Hotel so your bride won't catch her death. Pastor and I've taken the liberty of alerting your guests and arranging things at the hotel. My gift to you, dear boy."

For the second time today, Daniel was dumbfounded. "Thank you, sir. But Reagan may be preparing to leave this very minute." He took a step toward the door, but his elder stopped him.

289

"She's already been informed. Mrs. Goodwin has been with her all afternoon, as have several other women from the church. It's all in order, son. I have the carriage ready to escort you to your wedding. Shall we?"

What could he say? "Thank you, sir. This is most generous."

Mr. Goodwin patted him on the arm. "You are like a son to me, and as my additional wedding gift, I have reserved the presidential suite at the Crossmon for you— the very room where Mrs. Ulysses S. Grant stayed back in 1883. That way, you can enjoy your first night together in warmth and comfort without you lifting a finger." Mr. Goodwin cleared his throat, but his grin betrayed the meaning of his words.

"Sir, you honor me with your kindness." Daniel's voice came out husky with emotion, due to a very large lump in his throat.

Mr. Goodwin placed his hand on the doorknob. "Shall we go and meet your bride?"

Daniel agreed. He banked the fire, blew out the candle, and followed his benefactor to the waiting carriage. Anticipation kept him warm in the storm.

*This will be a night to remember!*

~ ~ ~

Reagan enjoyed every moment of the pampering she received from Mrs. Goodwin, the pastor's wife, and three other matrons of the church. They fawned over her like doting grandmothers, primping her hair, sharing their stories of wedded bliss, encouraging her as a bride. One woman shared pearl earbobs; another a pearl necklace; yet another her blue handkerchief, intricately embroidered with white hearts and the words, "I will love thee always."

As Mrs. Perkins thrust the handkerchief into her hands, she planted a kiss on her cheek. "Something old, something new, something borrowed, something blue. You are the tenth bride to borrow this, and each one has had such good fortune in their marriage. Why, I've counted thirty-six babies from these brides thus far." She winked at Reagan. "And, I'm sure, more to come."

Reagan's face grew warm as she thanked her. She thought she'd be alone on this stormy day. But this town had become her home, and these people, her people. In four short months, she'd found more love and support than she'd ever known.

Here, in this tiny hamlet of Alexandria Bay, she discovered community. People who cared for and sacrificed for one another. She found love, in the heart of a godly man who shared her faith and loved her deeply. In the eyes of little children eager to learn. In the faces of fellow parishioners and her students' families as they passed her on the street. In the kindness of the Bernheims in giving them a honeymoon in New York City, where her family would finally be able to meet her beloved.

A gentle knock drew her out of her reverie as Mrs. Goodwin opened the door.

Mr. Goodwin tipped his hat. "Good evening, ladies. The pastor and the groom are awaiting the bride in the ballroom." The older man tossed Reagan a wink. "See you downstairs." He gave his wife a peck on the cheek before hurrying down the hallway.

Reagan giggled as she pinched her cheeks. "I'm ready. I am so very ready!"

The other women cackled on their way out of the room, leaving only Reagan and Mrs. Goodwin. The older woman slipped her arm in the crook of Reagan's and waved a hand toward the door. "Shall we?"

Reagan sucked in a breath. Finally. Finally, she would become Mrs. Daniel Lovitz!

~ ~ ~

Daniel quivered with excitement as he waited at the makeshift altar in the Grand Ballroom of the Crossmon Hotel. The grandeur of the atmosphere made for a most magical place to get married, far more luxurious than the tiny church he'd planned on. But then, God seemed to be full of marvels of late. And why should that surprise him? Since he met Reagan, since he met God, his life had taken on more meaning, more joy, more love than he'd ever known.

He glanced at the guests, pleased that so many had ventured out in the snow to celebrate with them. Reagan's schoolchildren and their families took the front rows, the pupils wiggling in their seats. Other benevolent community members filled the back chairs. Mr. Goodwin stood beside him as Pastor Mark flipped through his Bible.

Just then, the doors opened and the crowd fell silent, save several deep gasps and a few titters from the elderly matrons and widows. There stood his bride, a wide smile beaming her joy, twinkling eyes brighter than the electric lights that lit the ballroom. Her elegant attire only framed the allure he beheld, for it was the woman whose beauty came from deep inside, from the heart, from the heavens above, that captivated him.

A prayer of thanksgiving danced in his mind as his eyes trained on Reagan. He thought it an eternity before she reached him, but finally, she arrived at his side. She let go of the arm of Mrs. Goodwin and handed her the bridal bouquet. Then she took his hands in hers.

"Dearly beloved …" Pastor Mark droned on and on as they moved through the service and said their vows.

Daniel hardly comprehended the nuptials yet somehow played his part flawlessly. He even remembered his mother's ring and thrilled at putting on his bride's finger.

All he could think of was that the God of the universe had seen fit to give him with a bride who was far more precious than the pearls she wore, a godly woman of character and dignity, a woman of excellence. A reward beyond measure.

# THE END!

# ABOUT THE AUTHOR

**Susan G Mathis** is an award-winning, multi-published author of stories set in the beautiful Thousand Islands, her childhood stomping ground in upstate NY. Her first two books of The Thousand Islands Gilded Age series, *Devyn's Dilemma* and *Katelyn's Choice* are available now, and she's working on book three. *The Fabric of Hope: An Irish Family Legacy*, *Christmas Charity*, and *Sara's Surprise* are also available. Susan's books have won numerous awards, including the Illumination Book Award, the American Fiction Award, and the Indie Excellence Book Award. Visit www.SusanGMathis.com for more.

Susan is also a published author of two premarital books with her husband, Dale, two children's picture books, a dozen stories in compilation books, and hundreds of published articles. Before Susan jumped into the fiction world, she served as the Founding Editor of *Thriving Family* magazine and the former Editor/Editorial Director of 12 Focus on the Family publications. Her first two published books were nonfiction, co-authored with her husband, Dale. *Countdown for Couples: Preparing for the Adventure of Marriage* with an Indonesian and Spanish version, and *The ReMarriage Adventure: Preparing for a Life of Love and Happiness*, have helped thousands of couples prepare for marriage. Susan is also the author of two children's picture books, *Lexie's Adventure in Kenya* and *Princess Madison's Rainbow Adventure*. Moreover, she is published in various book compilations including five *Chicken Soup for the Soul* books, *Ready to Wed*, *Supporting Families Through Meaningful Ministry*, *The Christian Leadership Experience*, and *Spiritual Mentoring of Teens*. Susan has also several hundred magazine and newsletter articles.

Susan is vice president of Christian Authors Network (CAN) and a member of American Christian Fiction Writers (ACFW). For over twenty years, Susan has been a speaker at writers' conferences, teachers' conventions, writing groups, and other organizational gatherings. Susan makes her home in Colorado Springs, enjoys traveling globally and relishes each time she gets to see or FaceTime with her four granddaughters.

# BOOKS BY SUSAN G MATHIS

Visit: www.SusanGMathis.com

## *Devyn's Dilemma*
### Book 2 of the Thousand Islands Gilded Age series
Heritage Beacon Fiction (2020) ISBN-13: 978-1645262732

     Devyn McKenna is forced to work in the Towers on Dark Island, one of the enchanting Thousand Islands. But when Devyn finds herself in service to the wealthy Frederick Bourne family, her life takes an unexpected turn.
     Brice McBride is Mr. Bourne's valet as well as the occasional tour guide and under butler. Brice tries to help the mysterious Devyn find peace and love in her new world, but she can't seem to stay out of trouble—especially when she's accused of stealing Bourne's money for Vanderbilt's NYC subway expansion.

## *Katelyn's Choice*
### Book 1 of the Thousand Islands Gilded Age series
Heritage Beacon Fiction (2019) 978-1946016720

Katelyn Kavanagh's mother dreamed her daughter would one day escape the oppressive environment of their Upstate New York farm for service in the enchanting Thousand Islands, home to Gilded Age millionaires. But when her wish comes true, Katelyn finds herself in the service of none other than the famous George Pullman, and the transition proves anything but easy.

Thomas O'Neill, brother of her best friend, is all grown up and also working on Pullman Island. Despite Thomas' efforts to help the irresistible Katelyn adjust to the intricacies of her new world, she just can't seem to tame her gossiping tongue—even when the information she's privy to could endanger her job, the 1872 re-election of Pullman guest President Ulysses S. Grant, and the love of the man of her dreams.

### *Peyton's Promise*, Book 3 coming 2022

~ ~ ~

### *Sara's Surprise*
**An Irish Brides novella, book 2**
smWordWorks (2019) 978-1087235714

Katelyn's best friend, Sara O'Neill, works as an assistant pastry chef at the magnificent Thousand Islands Crossmon Hotel where she meets precocious, seven-year-old Madison and her charming father and hotel manager, Sean Graham. But Jacque LaFleur, the pastry chef Sara works under, makes her dream job a nightmare.

Sean has trouble keeping Madison out of mischief and his mind off Sara. Though he finds Sara captivating, he's jealous of LaFleur and misreads Sara's desire to learn from the pastry chef as love. Can Sean learn to trust her and can Sara trust him—and herself to be an instant mother?

## *Christmas Charity*
### An Irish Brides novella, book 1
smWordWorks (2017) 978-0578207797

Susan Hawkins and Patrick O'Neill find that an arranged marriage is much harder than they think, especially when they emigrate from Wolfe Island, Canada, to Cape Vincent, New York, in 1864, just a week after they marry—with Patrick's nine-year-old daughter, Lizzy, in tow. Can twenty-three-year-old Susan Hawkins learn to love her forty-nine-year-old husband and find charity for her angry stepdaughter? With Christmas coming, she hopes so.

## *The Fabric of Hope: An Irish Family Legacy*
smWordWorks (2017) 978-1542890861

An 1850s Irish immigrant and a 21$^{st}$-century single mother are connected by faith, family, and a quilt. Will they both find hope for the future? After struggling to accept the changes forced upon her, Margaret Hawkins and her family take a perilous journey on an 1851 immigrant ship to the New World, bringing with her an Irish family quilt she is making. A hundred and sixty years later, her great granddaughter, Maggie, searches for the family quilt after her ex pawns it. But on their way to creating a family legacy, will these women find peace with the past and embrace hope for the future, or will they be imprisoned by fear and faithlessness?

## Other books by Susan G Mathis

*Countdown for Couples: Preparing for the Adventure of Marriage*

*The ReMarriage Adventure: Preparing for a Lifetime of Love & Happiness*

*Lexie's Adventure in Kenya, a children's picture book*

*Princess Madison's Rainbow Adventure, a children's picture book*

Susan is also an author in various book compilations including five *Chicken Soup for the Soul* books, *Ready to Wed, Supporting Families Through Meaningful Ministry,* and several more.

Visit her at www.SusanGMathis.com
sign up for her newsletter
and please consider writing an Amazon review.
Thanks!

Made in the USA
Monee, IL
04 November 2020

46574023R00167